The
Mr Pink-Whistle
Stories

The
Mr Pink-Whistle
Stories

The Mr Pink-Whistle Stories

Enid Blyton

Illustrations by Kevin Kimber

BLOOMSBURY
CHILDREN'S
BOOKS

First published by Parragon Publishing in 1999
Queen Street House, 4/5 Queen Street, Bath BA1 1HE

The Adventures of Mr Pink-Whistle was first published by Newnes in 1941
First published by Bloomsbury Publishing Plc in 1997
38 Soho Square, London, W1V 5DF
Mr Pink-Whistle Interferes was first published by Dean's International Publishing Ltd in 1949
Mr Pink-Whistle's Party was first published by George Newnes in 1955
First published by Bloomsbury Publishing Plc in 1998
38 Soho Square, London, W1V 5DF

Enid Blyton™

A CIP catalogue record of this book is available from the British Library

ISBN 1 84164 094 8

Printed in Scotland by Caledonian International Book Manufacturing Ltd

10 9 8 7 6 5 4 3 2 1

Contents

The Adventures of
  Mr Pink-Whistle   7

Mr Pink-Whistle Interferes   129

Mr Pink-Whistle's Party   241

The Adventures of Mr Pink-Whistle

The Adventures of Mr Pink-Whistle

Enid Blyton

Illustrations by Kevin Kimber

BLOOMSBURY
CHILDREN'S
BOOKS

Contents

1	The Little Secret Man	13
2	Mr Pink-Whistle Puts Things Right	23
3	The Girl with the Broken Doll	33
4	A Marvellous Afternoon	43
5	The Dog Who Lost his Collars	56
6	A Surprise for Dame Gentle	64
7	The Two Ugly Creatures	75
8	The Forgotten Rabbits	86
9	Jimmy's Day in the Country	97
10	The Mean Little Boy	108
11	Wilfrid Has a Good Many Shocks	117

Chapter 1

The Little Secret Man

'It isn't fair,' shouted Mr Pink-Whistle, 'it isn't fair!'

He stamped round the room in a rage, and his big black cat looked at him in alarm, and put her tail under her, out of his way.

'Here I've just been reading about a poor man who saved up and bought a nice new teapot for his wife – and on his way home a boy on roller-skates banged into him and broke his precious teapot!'

Mr Pink-Whistle put his hands under the back of his coat, pursed up his lips, and looked at his cat. 'Now is that fair, Sooty?' he shouted. 'Is that fair? Did anybody buy him another teapot? No! And look here – here's a picture of a little girl who ran to pick up something for a friend, and was knocked over by a car! Now, I ask you, Sooty – is *that* fair?'

'No-ee-oh-ee-ow,' answered Sooty in surprise.

'Well, I don't think it's fair either!' said Mr Pink-Whistle. 'I do think that if people are kind, they should be rewarded, not punished – and what's more, Sooty, I'm going to do something about it.'

'Oh-ee-ow!' said Sooty, waving her tail a little.

'Sooty, you know that I'm rather a lonely

little man, don't you?' said Mr Pink-Whistle
with a sigh; and he stroked his big black cat,
who began to purr at once.

'You see, Sooty, I'm not like ordinary people,' went on the little man, sinking down
into a chair. 'I haven't any real friends
except you. The reason is that I'm half a
brownie and half a proper person – so the
brownies don't like me much, and ordinary
people are afraid of me because I've got
brownie ears and green eyes like you.'

'R-r-r-r-r-r-r,' purred Sooty softly. She
knew how kind her master was, even if he
was only a half-and-half.

'*But,* Sooty, I've got a secret!' whispered
Mr Pink-Whistle into his black cat's pointed
ear. 'Yes, I've got a secret that I've never used
yet. I can make myself invisible whenever I
like!'

Sooty didn't know what Mr Pink-Whistle
meant. She stared at him out of eyes as
green as her master's.

'I'll show you what I mean, Sooty!' said Mr
Pink-Whistle. He shut his eyes and mur-
mured a few strange words that made Sooty
tremble and shiver.

And then Mr Pink-Whistle disappeared!

One moment he was there – and the next he was gone. Sooty blinked her eyes and looked all round the little warm kitchen.

Her green eyes nearly fell out of her head in surprise. Where, oh, where had Mr Pink-Whistle gone?

Sooty heard a faint giggle – and there was Mr Pink-Whistle back again! Sooty put her ears back and looked alarmed. 'Mee-ow-ee-ow!' she said. She hoped her master wasn't going to do this sort of thing very often.

'Now, that's my secret,' said Mr Pink-Whistle, pleased. 'And what I'm going to do, Sooty-cat, is to go into the big town and look out for unlucky people. I shall go into their houses, and I shall disappear into thin air, so that they don't know I'm there. And I shall see that they get a reward for being kind! What do you think of that for a good idea, Sooty?'

'Wow-ee-ow,' answered Sooty.

'You'll stay here and keep house for me,' said Mr Pink-Whistle, 'and I'll come back and see you often. Now I'll pack my bag and go. I won't let unfair things happen to people. I won't! I won't! I may be only a half-and-half, but I'll just show the world what I can do!'

He packed his bag, rubbed his face against Sooty's soft head, ran out of the front door, and waved goodbye.

Sooty watched her kind, funny little master go, and wondered what he would do.

'He won't be happy away from his cosy little home,' said Sooty. 'I know he won't. I wonder whose house he will go to?'

Now, in the nearest town lived a hard-working little woman called Mrs Spink. She had four small children, and it was very hard to feed and dress them properly. They didn't have many treats, but they were good little things and didn't grumble.

One day they all came rushing home from school in excitement. There was Teddy, with blue eyes and golden hair; there was Eliza, with red curls; there was Harry, with golden curls; and there was Bonny, with a mop of dark hair like a sweep's brush. They tore into the kitchen and made Mrs Spink jump so much that she almost upset the pan.

'Mother! Mother! There's a party at school on Thursday and we're all to go!' cried Teddy.

'But you haven't got any nice clothes,' said Mrs Spink. 'Not any at all! You've only got the ones you have on.'

'Can't you wash them, Mother, and make them nice and clean?' asked Eliza, almost in tears at the thought of not going to the party. Why, they had never been to one before!

'Well, on Wednesday afternoon you must all go to bed, so that I can wash your clothes ready for the party the next day,' said their mother. 'That is the best I can do for you.'

Teddy, Eliza, Harry, and Bonny were quite willing to spend an afternoon in bed if only their mother would get their clothes ready for the party. Then she could wash them, iron them, and mend them.

So on Wednesday afternoon all the four children undressed, got into their ragged little night-clothes, and cuddled into bed, with books to read. Mrs Spink took the dirty clothes into the garden, set up her wash-tub, and began to wash all the clothes – socks, stockings, vests, knickers, shorts, shirts, petticoats, dresses, jerseys – goodness, what a lot of things there were!

Mrs Spink sang as she worked. She saw a funny little man with big ears and curious green eyes looking at her over the fence as she rubbed and scrubbed.

'Good-day,' he said; 'you sound happy!'

'Well, my four children are going to their first party tomorrow,' said Mrs Spink, squeezing the dirty water from a frock, 'and that's enough to make any mother happy! Poor little things, they don't have many treats. I'm just washing the only clothes they have, so that they can go clean and neat.'

When she looked up again, the funny little man was gone. That was strange, thought Mrs Spink. She hadn't seen him go! She pegged up all the clothes on the line, emptied her tub, and went indoors to get the tea.

And do you know, the line broke, and

down went all the clean clothes into the mud! Would you believe it!

Poor Mrs Spink! When she came out to see how the clothes were getting on, she could have cried. All of them were far dirtier than before!

'Well, well!' said Mrs Spink, in as cheerful a voice as she could manage. 'I'll just have to wash them all again, that's all!'

So she set to work once more, and put all the clothes into her wash-tub again. How she rubbed and scrubbed away! She didn't see the funny little green-eyed man again – but he was there, all the same, watching her. He was sitting on the fence, quite invisible.

'It isn't fair!' he muttered to himself. 'After she washed all those clothes so beautifully! No, it isn't fair!'

Mrs Spink couldn't mend the line. It was so rotten that she was afraid it might break again, so she took all the clean clothes and spread them out flat on the grass at the front of the house to dry. Dresses, petticoats, socks – they were all there, as clean as could be.

Mrs Spink went in to take the kettle off the fire, for she really felt she could do with a cup of tea. Mr Pink-Whistle slipped in behind her, though she didn't see him. He sat on a chair, and thought what a nice, clean little kitchen it was.

And then a dreadful thing happened. Two dogs came into the front garden, and what must they do but run all over those nice clean clothes! They didn't miss a single one! So when poor little Mrs Spink went out to get them, there they were all covered with dirty, muddy footmarks.

She didn't cry. She just stood and looked and gave a heavy sigh. But Mr Pink-Whistle cried! The tears rolled down his cheeks, because he was so sorry for Mrs Spink.

'It isn't fair!' he whispered to himself. 'She worked so hard – and it was all for her children. It just isn't fair!'

Mrs Spink gathered up all the clothes and put them into her wash-tub again. She washed them clean for the third time, and she hung them up on the big airer that swung from the kitchen ceiling. Then she went upstairs to see how the children were getting on.

'I'll have to iron your clothes in the morning,' she told them. 'First, the line fell down and then two dogs ran over the washing. It's all in the kitchen now. Nothing can happen to it there.'

But she was wrong. Something did! A big heap of soot tumbled down the chimney, and when Mr Pink-Whistle looked up at the clothes they were all black with the flying soot!

'How dare you!' cried Mr Pink-Whistle, shaking his fist at the soot. 'How dare you! Oh, I can't bear this! I can't. I must put it right; I must – I must!'

And out he rushed to put things right – funny old Pink-Whistle!

Chapter 2

Mr Pink-Whistle
Puts Things Right

Well, what do you think Mr Pink-Whistle meant to do? He meant to go and buy new clothes for all the four children! Good old Mr Pink-Whistle!

He was so upset to think that the clothes had been spoilt for the third time, after Mrs Spink had worked so hard and so cheerfully, that he had to blow his nose hard to keep from crying.

'It's not fair!' he kept saying. 'Why do these things happen when people try so hard? I won't have it! I shall put it right. It's no good being sorry about things if you don't do something to put them right!'

He quite forgot that he was invisible still, and that people couldn't see him. So, when he walked into a clothes shop and the door-bell rang, the girl there was most alarmed to hear a voice and to see nobody!

'I want to see some party clothes,' said Mr Pink-Whistle. 'For two little boys and two little girls.'

'Oooh!' said the shop girl, frightened, for she could still see nobody. 'There's somebody speaking and there's nobody here! Help! Help!'

'Oh, sorry!' said Mr Pink-Whistle, remembering that he couldn't be seen. At once he came back again, and his fat little body, big ears, and green eyes appeared in front of the surprised girl.

'Now don't run away or do anything silly,' said Mr Pink-Whistle. 'It's a secret I have – I can make myself disappear or not. Please show me the children's clothes you have.'

The girl looked into Mr Pink-Whistle's kind red face, and knew that he couldn't harm anyone. She took down some boxes and drew open some drawers. In a little while she and Mr Pink-Whistle were talking about what would be best for Teddy, Eliza, Harry, and Bonny to wear at the school party.

They chose new vests, warm and white. They chose knickers and socks, two pretty petticoats, two pairs of grey flannel shorts for the boys, and two blue silk frocks for the girls. Mr Pink-Whistle chose a green jersey for Harry and a red one for Teddy.

'Would that be all, do you think?' asked the girl, who was really quite enjoying herself now, for Mr Pink-Whistle had told her all about poor Mrs Spink, and she was feeling quite excited to think of the surprise that this funny little secret man was planning.

'Well – what about hair-ribbons for the two girls to match their frocks?' asked Mr Pink-Whistle. 'Or don't girls wear them now?'

'Oh, of course they do!' said the shop girl,

and she measured and cut two fine hair-ribbons of blue silk for Eliza and Bonny. 'Oh, and have the children shoes, sir? Did those get spoilt too?'

'Well, Mrs Spink didn't wash the shoes,' said Mr Pink-Whistle. 'But I remember seeing them in the kitchen – very poor old shoes, too. I'd better have four pairs, I think.'

So they chose brown shoes that they thought would fit the children – and then that was really all. The girl did everything up in a big parcel and gave it to Mr Pink-Whistle. They beamed at one another, pleased to think of the secret they both shared.

Mr Pink-Whistle paid for the things. Then he said goodbye and went. He ran straight back to Mrs Spink's. He nearly forgot to make himself disappear, but just remembered in time. Then he opened the door and marched in, unseen by anyone.

Mrs Spink was still upstairs with her children. She didn't know anything about the sooty clothes downstairs yet. Mr Pink-Whistle looked round the black kitchen and frowned.

'I can't put the children's clothes here,' he

thought. 'They would get sooty. What about the next room?'

Now in the next room was a big chest of drawers where Mrs Spink kept all the clothes of the family, and all the sheets and towels. Mr Pink-Whistle tiptoed to it and pulled the drawers open. The top one and the bottom one were empty. So Mr Pink-Whistle carefully and neatly put the boys' clothes into the top drawer and the girls' clothes into the bottom one. They looked lovely. Mr Pink-Whistle felt very happy as he packed them in.

Mrs Spink ran down the stairs to the kitchen. When she saw the sooty clothes and the black kitchen, she gave a cry of horror. And then, because she was so tired, she sat down on a sooty chair and began to weep.

'My beautiful washing!' she wept. 'Oh, I did think nothing more would happen to it! I'm too tired to do it again – but what will the poor children say if they've no clean clothes to wear at the party tomorrow? Oh dear! Oh dear! Things are very hard!'

The children came running down the stairs to see what was the matter with their mother. Mr Pink-Whistle watched them from

the other room. Would they be angry?
Would they be sulky – or very, very sad?

When they saw what had happened they

were full of dismay and horror, for they knew
that their poor mother had already washed
the clothes three times. They flung their
arms around her and hugged her.

'You won't be able to go to the party, my
dears!' wept their mother. 'I'm too tired to
wash the clothes again.'

'Mother, *we* don't mind!' cried Teddy.

'Mother, it doesn't matter a bit!' cried

Eliza.

'Don't you cry, Mother; we'll help you wash again tomorrow,' promised little Bonny.

'We don't mind about the party!' cried Harry, though he did really mind, dreadfully.

'Nice children, kind children!' said tender-hearted Mr Pink-Whistle to himself, feeling for his handkerchief again. 'Oh, I'm glad I'm here to do something! I can't bear things like this to happen!'

'You're the best children in the world!' said their mother, and kissed them all. 'And that's just why you, of all children, should have a treat. It isn't fair!'

'No, it's not!' said Mr Pink-Whistle in a loud whisper. The children heard it, and looked surprised. Mr Pink-Whistle thought it was time that they saw what he had done for them, and he pulled open the top drawer and rattled it a little.

'What's that noise?' said Mrs Spink in surprise. 'I hope the cat isn't in my parlour, messing things up!'

They all went into the little parlour. They didn't see Mr Pink-Whistle of course, because he was invisible, but they bumped into him without knowing it!

'Who has opened this top drawer?' wondered Mrs Spink, catching sight of the half-opened drawer. She went to shut it – and then she stared – and stared – and stared!

'Look!' she said in amazement, and pulled out of the drawer all the new socks, jerseys, vests and shorts belonging to the boys. 'New clothes! And new shoes too! Good gracious! Where did they come from!'

The girls pulled open the other drawers and soon found their new clothes in the bottom drawer. How they squealed and shrieked when they saw their blue frocks and ribbons to match!

In a trice the four children dressed themselves. Mr Pink-Whistle had guessed their sizes exactly. They all looked as sweet as could be, and if Mr Pink-Whistle had been their father he couldn't have felt prouder of them all.

'I don't understand it, I don't understand it!' said Mrs Spink, thinking she must be in a lovely dream.

'Now don't be frightened,' said Mr Pink-Whistle suddenly, 'because I'm going to *appear*. One, two, three – and here I am!'

And there he was! All five looked at him in astonishment. 'Did *you* put those new clothes there?' asked Mrs Spink.

'Yes, I did,' said Mr Pink-Whistle. 'I'm tired of seeing and hearing and reading about things going wrong in this world. I can't bear it! It's not fair! So I'm just taking a little holiday to put some of the things right. And I was so upset about your having to wash those clothes so often that I felt I *must* go and buy some new ones. I do hope you don't mind.'

'You're a darling!' cried Bonny, and she

suddenly hugged him. It was the first time Mr Pink-Whistle had ever been hugged and he thought it was lovely.

'Well, this is my first try at putting things right,' he said. 'I'm glad it is a success. Now be sure you enjoy your party tomorrow, my dears!'

'We couldn't help enjoying it, with all these fine clothes!' cried Eliza, dancing round the room in her blue silk. 'Thank you, dear kind little man!'

Mr Pink-Whistle felt so happy that he thought he would burst. He hurriedly muttered the magic words that made him invisible again, and he disappeared. 'Goodbye!' he cried. 'Goodbye! I'll come and see you again sometime. I'm off to find something else to put right. Goodbye!'

'Goodbye!' cried the children, wondering where their peculiar, green-eyed friend had gone. He was off through the falling night, as happy as could be.

'Now for something else!' he said, with a skip and a jump. 'Now for something else!'

And he'll find it all right, as you'll very soon see!

Chapter 3

The Girl with
the Broken Doll

Well, Mr Pink-Whistle's next adventure was with a little girl who had a beautiful new doll. Her name was Jessie, and one day when she passed by the toy shop window, she saw the most lovely baby doll she had ever seen, sitting there looking at her.

The doll was dressed in woolly clothes, and had a round woollen hat on its head with a bobble at the top. Its eyes were wide open and had long lashes. Its mouth smiled, and it had tiny little shining nails on its fingers and toes.

Jessie stood still and looked at the doll for a very long time. She loved it with all her heart. She longed to have it in her arms to hold. She longed to put it to bed in her toy cot.

'How much is that doll, Mummy?' she asked.

'It is very expensive,' said her mother, looking at the ticket on it. 'It is ten pounds. Don't ask me to buy it for you, because I haven't even got one pound to spare!'

'No, I won't ask you, Mummy,' said Jessie. She turned away from the doll, and went home. But all the time she was having tea she remembered the doll's face and how its big brown eyes had looked at her, with their long curling lashes. And when she was in bed that night she remembered the doll again and wished she had it with her to cuddle.

'I shall save up, and save up, and save up till I have ten pounds,' said Jessie to herself. 'Mummy says if you want a thing badly enough you can get it in the end, somehow! So I will get that lovely doll. Its name shall be Rosemary Ann. Sometimes I shall call her Rosemary and sometimes I shall call her Ann!'

Then Jessie began to save up. She saved all her Saturday ten pences. She saved one pound that she had for her birthday. She saved fifty pence that Uncle Fred gave her and twenty pence that Aunt Flo gave her. Every time Mummy gave her ten pence for running an errand or helping, she put that into her money-box too. She didn't spend anything on sweets.

She found twenty pence in the street one day, and as she couldn't find out who had lost it, Mummy let her put that in her money-box too. And at last, after three whole months, she had ten pounds!

'This is the most exciting day of my life,' said Jessie to her mother that morning. 'I am going to buy that new doll for my very own.

She is to be called Rosemary Ann. She has such a lovely face, Mummy, and you should just see her dear little finger-nails and toe-nails!'

Jessie got the cot ready for her new doll. She found a doll's cup and saucer for her to drink from. She got ready her doll's pram to fetch Rosemary Ann from the shop. Then she put her ten pounds into her bag and set off happily, thinking joyfully of the lovely doll that would so soon be hers.

There it was, still sitting in the window. Jessie ran inside the door, put down her money, and bought the doll. And at that very moment Mr Pink-Whistle came along, looking for an adventure! He couldn't be seen, for he was quite invisible. He wouldn't let himself be seen in the town if he could help it, because people laughed at his big ears and green eyes.

He saw Jessie's happy face and was pleased. He followed her into the shop without anyone knowing. He saw the little girl buy her doll. He watched her take it into her arms and hold it there lovingly.

'You feel beautiful,' said Jessie to the doll. 'Your name is Rosemary Ann. I saved up for

you for three whole months. I didn't buy any
sweets. I didn't spend even five pence,
because I wanted you so badly. And now, you
darling Rosemary, I've got you! You're mine!
There's a cosy cot waiting for you at home,
and a chair, and a cup and saucer – and
there's your pram outside ready to take you
home!'

The doll looked up at Jessie out of her big
eyes. Jessie pulled the woolly hat straight and
hugged Rosemary.

'I'm happier than I've ever been in my
life!' she said. Mr Pink-Whistle beamed all
over his red face. This was what he liked to
hear. So many people were sad or hurt or
disappointed, but now here was someone
happy. He followed Jessie out of the shop
and watched her tuck the doll up carefully in
the blue pram. Then Jessie took the handle
and began to push the pram proudly home,
hoping that people would look into it and
see the fine new doll.

But almost at once a dreadful thing happened. A crowd of boys came along with a
big dog. They were shouting and laughing,
and the dog was very excited. It kept jumping all around the boys and trying to lick

their faces.

And just as the boys and the dog reached Jessie, the dog jumped up to one of the boys, fell sideways, and knocked Jessie's little blue pram right over!

Rosemary Ann was jerked out on to her head. There was a loud crack, and Jessie gave a scream.

'Rosemary! Oh, Rosemary's broken!' The little girl picked up her poor doll, and looked in horror at the broken face. The nose was smashed, and the lovely eyes had gone inside Rosemary's head. She was quite, quite spoilt.

'I say! I'm sorry our dog did that!' said one of the boys. 'It was quite an accident. Shall we scold the dog?'

'Oh no,' said poor Jessie, with hot tears trickling down her cheeks. 'Don't scold him. He didn't mean to do it. Oh, I'm so unhappy. I've only just this minute bought Rosemary Ann, and I saved up for three whole months to buy her. And now she's broken, the poor, poor thing!'

'Perhaps your mother will buy you another one,' said a boy.

'I shan't ask her to,' said Jessie, wiping her

eyes. 'She hasn't got much money.'

The boys ran off with their dog and soon forgot about Jessie. Mr Pink-Whistle was left, standing invisible beside the pram. He was terribly upset. He sniffed so loudly that Jessie heard him and looked around. But she couldn't see anyone, of course.

Mr Pink-Whistle felt angry and upset and sad and unhappy all at once. He walked round the corner and stamped up and down in a rage. 'It isn't fair! It isn't fair! That's a dear little girl, and she saved up so hard, and did so love the doll, and then the dog came and broke it. Now she's very, very unhappy. And the doll's broken so much that it can't be mended. What am I to do to put it right? It really isn't fair, and I won't have it!'

Suddenly Mr Pink-Whistle knew what to do. He made himself appear suddenly, much to a small boy's surprise, and rushed into the toy shop. He banged on the counter. The shop woman appeared and looked surprised to see a fat little man wiping his green eyes with an enormous yellow handkerchief.

'Have you got another doll like the one the little girl bought just now?' he asked.

'Oh yes, of course,' said the shop woman, and she lifted one out of the box. Mr Pink-Whistle snatched it up, slammed down the money, and tore out. The shop woman really thought he was quite mad.

Jessie was walking home with her pram. She had put poor broken Rosemary Ann into it again, with her face towards the pillow, so that she couldn't see how broken she was.

Mr Pink-Whistle hurried up, and just as he got near, he dropped two or three pennies. They went rolling all over the place. 'Dear, dear!' said Mr Pink-Whistle, pretending to be vexed. 'Now where have they gone?'

'I'll get them for you,' said Jessie, just as he had known she would. She put her pram by the side of the pavement, and went to pick up the pennies. As quick as lightning Mr Pink-Whistle whipped the broken doll out of the pram and put the new one in, face downwards. He stuffed the broken one into one of his big pockets, and covered up the other doll.

Soon Jessie came up to give him the pennies. 'What's the matter with your doll?' he asked. 'Why do you make her lie face downwards?'

'Because she's broken,' said Jessie, nearly crying again.

'Now, how lucky that is!' said Mr Pink-Whistle. 'I can mend broken dolls! Look! I just tap her on the back of the head gently – like this – and say "Hi-tiddle-hi-to, hi-tiddle-hi-to!" And hey presto! – the doll will be all right again!'

Jessie didn't believe him. She knew dolls weren't mended like that. But to please the funny little man she turned her doll over – and then she gave a scream.

'Rosemary Ann! You *are* all right! Your nose has come back! Your eyes are looking at me! You're quite, quite well! Oh, you darling! I'm so happy!' She snatched the doll out of the pram and hugged it as if she would squeeze it to bits. Mr Pink-Whistle felt all funny about the eyes again, and blew his nose loudly. This was fun! He'd put something right again! Good!

'Thank you ever so much,' said Jessie, her eyes shining with happiness. 'You must be magic!'

'I am, a bit,' said Mr Pink-Whistle, and his big ears waggled like a dog's and his green eyes gleamed. 'Well goodbye, little friend! Don't forget me, will you?'

'Oh, never!' said Jessie. 'I think you're really wonderful!'

So no wonder Mr Pink-Whistle skipped off as if he were treading on air. 'I've done it again! And I'll do it a third time before I'm much older! Yes, I certainly will.'

Chapter 4

A Marvellous Afternoon

Jackie Brown was so excited that he could hardly keep still. He kept hopping about, first on one foot and then on another, till his mother told him to go out into the garden and hop there, on the smooth green grass.

'I shall be a grasshopper then!' said Jackie. 'Oh, Mother, I'm so excited! Tomorrow I'm going to see the conjurer at the flower show. There's a great big tent there, and for twenty pence everyone can go in and see the conjurer. I've got twenty pence and I'm going!'

'You've told me that about twenty times already!' said his mother, laughing. 'Go along out and play, and just think of something else for a change!'

But Jackie couldn't think of anything else. He had seen a conjurer once before, and the magic things he did were so wonderful that the little boy had never forgotten them. Fancy, he even made a rabbit come out of an empty glove! Jackie had known it was empty, because it was his own glove that he had lent to the conjurer!

'And tomorrow the conjurer will do lots more magic!' said the little boy happily. 'Oh, shan't I enjoy it!'

He saw Eileen and Dick next door, and he climbed over the wall to play with them. Dick had a new kite and he was trying to fly it. It was a lovely one.

The wind suddenly took it up very high, and Dick squealed with delight. 'Look at it!' he shouted. 'It's flying like a bird!'

But it didn't fly like a bird for long. The wind dropped and down came the kite – and it fell on top of the greenhouse! Dick tugged it. It was stuck tightly.

'Oh, bother!' he said. 'It's stuck! What shall I do?'

Jackie took the string and pulled gently. It was no use, the kite was held fast by something. 'Wait till the gardener comes, and

he'll get a ladder and get it down for you,'
he said.

'I did want to fly it this afternoon with
Uncle Harry,' said Dick. 'He promised to
take me to the hills.'

'Well, perhaps I can get it for you if the
ladder isn't too heavy to carry,' said Jackie.
He found the ladder, and the three children
carried it carefully to the greenhouse. They
set it up at the back, and Jackie went up the
rungs.

He came to the kite. The string was wound
round the spike at the top of the greenhouse. Jackie pulled hard, and then let go of
the top of the ladder to undo the string.

The ladder wobbled – the ladder fell!
Crash! Jackie and the ladder reached the
ground together! Poor Jackie! He banged
his head so hard on the ground that for a
moment he couldn't get up. He felt peculiar.
Then he sat up and held his head.

'You've cut your head on a stone,' said
Eileen, frightened. 'It's bleeding. Come and
show my mother, quickly.'

It was such a bad cut that Jackie had to
have his head carefully bathed and bound
up in a bandage. The little boy had had a

bad shock, and his mother called in the doctor.

'The cut will soon heal,' said kind Doctor Henry. 'But he must be kept very quiet indeed for a day or two, Mrs Brown, to get over the shock. Put him to bed.'

'Oh, I can't go to bed – I can't, I can't!' wept poor Jackie. 'I want to see the conjurer tomorrow at the flower show. Oh, please let me go!'

'I'm afraid you wouldn't enjoy yourself a bit, if you went all the way to the flower show and back, with that dreadful aching head of yours,' said Doctor Henry. 'Be a good boy and lie quietly, and you'll soon be right. The conjurer will come again next year, I expect.'

'But next year is so far away!' wept Jackie, more disappointed than he had ever been in his life before. 'My head feels all right, really it does. Oh, I do want to go and see the conjurer! I'm so unhappy! All I did was to try and help Dick get his kite down – and now I've got a most unfair punishment, because I'm not to have my treat.'

'It's very bad luck, old man,' said the doctor. 'Very bad luck. But these things do sometimes happen, you know.'

'It shouldn't have happened when I was doing somebody a good turn,' wept Jackie.

'No, it shouldn't,' said the doctor. 'You deserved a better reward than this!'

Poor Jackie! He was put to bed and there he had to stay. Dick and Eileen knew all about it next day, and they were very sad indeed. 'Just because he tried to get down my kite!' said Dick gloomily. 'It isn't fair!'

A small fat man, with strange big ears and bright green eyes like a cat's, was passing by when Dick said these words. He stopped at once.

'What isn't fair?' he asked.

Dick told him all about Jackie, and how he had hurt himself doing a kind deed, and now couldn't go to see the marvellous conjurer.

'He's very unhappy about it,' said Eileen. 'We've sent him some books to read, and I've lent him my best jigsaw puzzle – but I'm sure he'll cry all the afternoon when the time comes for the flower show.'

'Too bad, too bad!' said Mr Pink-Whistle – because, as you have guessed, he was the little fat man! 'I can't bear things like this, and I just won't have them. I shall put this right somehow!'

The two children stared in surprise at Mr Pink-Whistle. There was something very strange about him – and in a minute there was something even stranger still, because he just simply wasn't there! He had vanished before their very eyes!

'Where's he gone?' said Eileen in great surprise.

You would be surprised to know where he had gone! He had crept up to a rabbit-hole in the field nearby and had made a noise like a juicy carrot. Up came a tiny fat baby rabbit – and Mr Pink-Whistle caught it and put it into his pocket. Then he went back to Jackie's house. Nobody could see him, of course.

He climbed up a pipe and looked in at a window.

In the bedroom there was a small boy lying in bed with his head bandaged up, and tears rolling down his white cheeks. It was Jackie, feeling very unhappy because it was the afternoon of the flower show and he couldn't go to see the conjurer.

Mr Pink-Whistle sighed. He hated to see anyone unhappy. He climbed quietly in at the window and stood looking at Jackie.

'Hello!' he said suddenly.

'Hello!' said Jackie in surprise, looking all round to see where the voice came from. There wasn't anyone he could see at all.

'I'm a conjurer, come to do a few tricks for you,' said Mr Pink-Whistle.

'Good gracious!' said Jackie astonished. 'But where are you! I can't see you!'

'Well, you see, I'm so magic that I'm invisible at present,' said Mr Pink-Whistle. 'Now just tell me a few things you'd like to hop from the mantelpiece on to your bed, and they'll come!'

Jackie giggled. It was funny to think of things hopping from the mantelpiece to his bed. 'I'd like the clock to come,' he said. At once the clock seemed to jump from the mantelpiece and land on Jackie's bed! Of course, it was really Mr Pink-Whistle carrying it, but, as Jackie couldn't see him, it looked as if the clock came by itself!

Then a china pig flew through the air and back again. The coal-shuttle did a little jigging dance round the room, all by itself –

though, of course, it was really Mr Pink-Whistle carrying it and jigging it about. But it did look so very funny!

Then Jackie's teddy bear stood on the rail at the foot of his bed and danced a comical dance, sticking his legs out just as if he were doing steps! Jackie laughed till he cried. He couldn't see Mr Pink-Whistle's hands holding the bear. He thought the bear really was doing it!

'Now ask any of your toys to speak to you, and hear them talk!' cried Mr Pink-Whistle, thoroughly enjoying himself. It was so lovely to make somebody happy.

'Well – I'd like my old toy soldier in that corner to say something to me,' said Jackie, sitting up in bed.

Mr Pink-Whistle, quite unseen, walked to where the soldier was sitting. He made it wave its hand to Jackie, and then he talked for it, in a sort of gruff voice.

'Hello, Jackie! Get better soon!'

'Oh, Soldier! I never knew you could talk before!' cried Jackie, very excited. 'Horsey, can you talk to me too?'

His old horse stood in the corner. Mr Pink-Whistle made it jiggle about, and then he spoke for it. 'Nay-hay-hay-hay-ay! Nay-hay-hay-hay-ay! Hurry up and get better and ride on me, Jackie! Nay-hay-hay-hay-ay!'

Jackie was thrilled. 'You've got a lovely, neighing voice, Horsey!' he said. 'Oh, what fun this is! How magic you are, Mr Conjurer!'

'Pink-Whistle is my name,' said Mr Pink-Whistle politely. 'I'm glad you like the magic I do.'

'I only wish you could make a rabbit come out of somewhere, like the other conjurer did,' sighed Jackie. 'That was really most surprising magic.'

Mr Pink-Whistle felt the little baby rabbit in his pocket, and he was delighted that he had thought of bringing it.

'Where would you like the rabbit to come from?' he asked.

'Oh, out of my bed!' said Jackie. 'It would be lovely to have a rabbit in bed with me! And Mr Pink-Whistle, couldn't I see you please? You sound the kindest, nicest person I've ever heard.'

'Do I really?' said Mr Pink-Whistle, feeling very happy. 'I'm glad. Well – you *shall* see me, Jackie. Just look at the clock on the mantelpiece for one whole minute, and at the end of it, look at the foot of your bed. I'll be there!'

Now whilst Jackie was busily watching the clock, waiting till a minute had gone by, Mr Pink-Whistle carefully and quickly put the tiny rabbit into Jackie's bed, at the foot. Then he said the words that made him appear, and just as Jackie had counted the whole minute, there was Mr Pink-Whistle grinning away at him at the foot of the bed, his green eyes shining brightly.

'Oh! How nice and funny and jolly you are!' cried Jackie – and then he gave a squeal, because something was creeping up his bed. He put his hand down – and pulled out a baby rabbit!

'You're more magic than the other conjurer!' shouted Jackie. 'You really are! You're – you're . . .'

And just then the door opened and Jackie's mother came in to see what the noise was. Mr Pink-Whistle disappeared just in time.

'Look! Look! A conjurer has been here, and he made this rabbit come out of my bed!' squealed Jackie. 'Oh, I'm so happy! It's my very own rabbit for me!'

'But there's no conjurer here!' said Jackie's mother in astonishment, looking all round. And yet – the rabbit was certainly there. How very, very strange!

A little giggle came from the window, out of which Mr Pink-Whistle was quietly climbing. Down he went – and off into the world again to find something else to put right. Hurry, Mr Pink-Whistle!

Chapter 5

The Dog Who
Lost his Collars

Now once Mr Pink-Whistle had a rather peculiar adventure. It was with a little terrier dog.

The dog's name was Jinky, and it lived with its master and mistress in a nice little house in the town. Jinky was a friendly dog, and loved to welcome people, and he was always ready to put out his small red tongue to lick anyone.

But now, week after week, he was in disgrace. His mistress and master scolded him hard. It was the first time, and he was very unhappy.

'You are a very bad little dog to keep losing your nice new collars!' his mistress said to him. 'You lost your first new red collar, and we bought you a green one with your name on it. You lost that the very next day! Then you had a fine brown one with bright studs all round it – and you came home without it the next week! And now you have lost the new blue one we gave you yesterday!'

'Woof!' said Jinky sadly.

'You are very naughty not to want to wear your collar,' said his master sternly. 'All dogs wear collars. So do their masters! You should be proud to be like your master! I can't imagine how you get your collar off, you bad dog – but just remember this, that you will be scolded and locked up in your kennel every time you do it!'

Jinky's master banged the kennel gate and left poor Jinky shut up inside. He was very sad. He lay and whined pitifully. It wasn't fair! He hadn't lost his collars! A horrid big boy had taken them away from him each time! But he couldn't tell his master that, because he could only talk doggy language, and no two-legged people understood it.

Just then somebody came by who *did* understand whines and yelps and barks. It was fat little Mr Pink-Whistle of course! He was half a brownie, and his big pointed ears could understand all that the birds and animals said, just as the real brownies could.

So Mr Pink-Whistle could hear all that poor Jinky was saying as he passed by the little house. To you and to me it might have sounded like 'Ooooo! Oooooo! Oooooo! Yelp, yelp, yelp! Oooooo! Oooooo!'

But to Mr Pink-Whistle it sounded like this:

'Oh, how sad I am! Oh, how unfair everything is! Oh, what a poor little dog I am, scolded for nothing! Oh, and how I love my master and mistress, and now I have made them very unhappy; but I couldn't help it, and they have made *me* unhappy too – but they *could* help it! Oh, tails and whiskers, I wish I wasn't a dog!'

Mr Pink-Whistle stopped and listened in astonishment. What could be the matter with the poor little dog? He made himself disappear and then he walked up the garden path and looked for the kennel. Inside was Jinky, his head on his paws, whining away to himself.

'What's the matter?' asked Mr Pink-Whistle in surprise. Jinky looked up. He couldn't see anyone, but he could smell somebody. How peculiar!

'It's all right,' said Mr Pink-Whistle, patting Jinky. 'I'm here, though you can't see me! Tell me, what's the matter?'

So Jinky told him his trouble. 'I'm being punished for something I didn't do,' he whined. 'But my master doesn't understand me when I try to tell him. A nasty, horrid boy keeps putting down lovely bones in the next street, and when I go to smell the bone, the boy pops out and catches me. Then he takes off my collar, and sends me home without it.'

'Well, what a wicked thing to do!' said Mr Pink-Whistle, very angry. 'And you've been scolded for that! Poor little dog, it's a shame! It's not fair! I must put it right.'

He undid the kennel gate and Jinky slipped out of his kennel and out of the yard into the garden. 'Now you come along with me,' said Mr Pink-Whistle. 'We'll go and find this boy. Keep at my heels. You can smell them, even if you can't see them! We'll do to that boy a little of what he has done to you.'

Together they trotted down the street and round the corner. People meeting them only saw a small dog with a new collar round his neck – but Mr Pink-Whistle was there all right too! But he couldn't be seen.

'Look!' said the dog, stopping. 'There's a lovely bone over there. I'm sure it's put there by that boy, so that I or any other dog shall go to it. Then he would catch us and steal our collars.'

'Well, you run up to it and smell it,' said Mr Pink-Whistle. 'Don't be afraid. I shall be near you.'

So Jinky ran up to the bone – and close beside him was Mr Pink-Whistle. As soon as Jinky reached the bone and sniffed at it, a big arm came over the fence and caught hold of the little dog. He was pulled right over the fence – and there behind the fence was a big boy with a horrid sly face.

'Another collar!' he grinned. But he didn't grin long! No – something most extra-ordinary happened!

Something took hold of him and wrenched at *his* collar! Something pulled at his tie. Something jerked at his coat – and before he could do anything to stop it, his collar, tie, and coat were taken right off him.

'Don't! What is it? Who is it? I can't see anyone!' cried the frightened boy. 'Go away! Go away!'

'I'm only doing to you what you've done to little dogs!' said a stern voice in his ear. 'Off with your shirt! Off with your boots! Off with your socks!'

Off came everything except the boy's vest and trousers!

'Next time you think of stealing anything, just think of Mr Pink-Whistle!' hissed a voice in his ear. 'Yes – Mr Pink-Whistle! I'll come after you again and take your clothes away if you dare to steal another collar from a dog!'

'Mr P-p-p-p-pink-Whistle, please give me b-b-b-b-ack my clothes!' wept the boy. 'My mother will scold me if I go home without them.'

'Good!' said Mr Pink-Whistle. 'Very good. Go home and get scolded then!'

And the angry little man pushed the naughty boy so that he almost fell on to his nose. He ran off, howling and crying, wondering fearfully who Mr Pink-Whistle was. He couldn't see him – but he was there all right!

Mr Pink-Whistle went to the nearest dustbin and stuffed the clothes in without being seen by anyone. Jinky licked his hand, after smelling about it for some time. The little dog thought Mr Pink-Whistle was wonderful.

'Now you go home, too,' said the fat little man, patting Jinky kindly. 'And don't be afraid of that boy any more. He's not likely to worry you or any other little dog again!'

Then off went Jinky very merrily, his tail in the air. Off went Mr Pink-Whistle too – and you may be sure that if he had had a tail it would have been straight up in the air as well, just like Jinky's!

Chapter 6

A Surprise For Dame Gentle

There was once an old woman called Dame Gentle, and she was just like her name. She was a dear old thing, and all the children loved her.

She was very poor, and sometimes, like Mother Hubbard, when she went to the cupboard – the cupboard was bare!

One day she had a bit of luck. Mrs Biddle wanted some scrubbing done, and she asked Dame Gentle if she thought she could do it.

'Of course!' said Dame Gentle. 'Haven't I rubbed and scrubbed all my life? A good bit of hard work never hurt anybody! I'll come along tomorrow and do whatever you want me to. Ah, I'm pleased about this, Mrs Biddle. I want a new blanket for my bed, and a new kettle for my stove. Maybe I'll be able to get them now!'

Well, she worked very hard indeed, and when the cleaning was done she had enough money to get what she wanted. She was very happy.

'Now for once I'll give myself a real treat!' said Old Dame Gentle. 'It's my birthday next week, and I'll make myself a cake, and get in a tin of cocoa to make some hot cocoa. I'll boil the water in my new kettle, and I'll be warm at night under my new blanket. Ah, I'm in luck's way just now!'

She asked Mother Dilly to come and share the cake and the cocoa with her, for she was a generous old thing. When the day came, Dame Gentle ran out to ask one of her neighbours for a few flowers to put on her table.

And whilst she was gone, who should come to the open door but Mister Mean! He rapped. Nobody answered. He pushed open the door a bit wider and looked inside. Dame Gentle was not there!

Then Mister Mean saw the new cake on the table, the tin of cocoa, and the new blanket set out ready to show Mother Dilly when she came. His mean little eyes gleamed with delight. He tiptoed into the kitchen, put the cake and the cocoa into his pockets, and rolled up the nice new blanket. He threw it over his shoulder and ran out of the room and down the path.

Just in time too – for Dame Gentle was coming back with a few flowers for the table. She trotted up the path to the front door, which she had left open, and walked into her warm kitchen.

'Mother Dilly will be here in a minute,' she thought. 'I wonder if that kettle's boiling.'

And then she saw that her beautiful new cake was gone! And the tin of cocoa! And the lovely warm blanket!

Dame Gentle stared as if she couldn't believe her eyes. *Where* had they gone to? She looked all round. She looked in the cupboard – but the cupboard was bare!

'Somebody's stolen them!' she said, and she sank down into her chair. 'Oh, how mean! To steal from an old, old woman like me! My lovely cake – and my beautiful blanket – all gone! What a horrid thing to happen on my birthday!'

There was a knock at the door and Mother Dilly walked in. 'What's the matter?' she cried, when she saw how sad Dame Gentle looked.

'Somebody has stolen all my birthday things, that I worked so hard to get,' said Dame Gentle, wiping her eyes. 'It's upset me a bit.'

'What a shame!' said Mother Dilly, putting her arms round her friend. 'Oh, what a shame! Who stole them?'

'I don't know,' said Dame Gentle. 'I just ran out to get those flowers, and when I came back everything was gone – even the tin of cocoa!'

'Now don't you cry, dear,' said her friend. 'I'll just run home and get a bit of tea, and two pieces of shortbread that I've got left in my tin. And we'll eat those for your birthday.'

She left the old woman and hurried out into the street, really angry to think that someone should have treated old Dame Gentle so badly. She bumped into a fat little man with curious green eyes, as she ran out of the gate.

'Oh, I beg your pardon!' said Mother Dilly. 'I'm feeling rather hot and angry, and I didn't look where I was going.'

'Hot and angry!' said Mr Pink-Whistle in surprise, for of course it was the little secret man who happened to be passing by. 'What's the matter?'

'Somebody has taken the cake, the cocoa, and the new blanket that my poor old friend, Dame Gentle, worked so hard to get,' said Mother Dilly fiercely. 'Isn't it a shame?'

'It certainly *is*!' said Mr Pink-Whistle,

pricking up his ears at once. 'Is she a kind old soul?'

'The kindest in the world!' said Mother Dilly. 'She doesn't deserve such bad luck. I'm sure it's that horrid Mister Mean who has done this. He is such a sly creature, and not at all honest.'

'Really?' said Mr Pink-Whistle. 'Where does he live?'

'He lives at Cherry Cottage, round the corner,' said Mother Dilly. The little fat man raised his hat and ran off. Mother Dilly wondered who he was and what he was going to do.

Mr Pink-Whistle made himself disappear when he turned the corner. Then quite invisible, he looked for Cherry Cottage. Ah – there it was, at the end. He walked quietly up the path and looked in at the window.

Mister Mean was there, grinning away to himself. He had got the cake on the table, and had already eaten half of it. He had made himself a fine jug of hot cocoa from the cocoa powder in the tin, and he had draped the new blanket round himself to see how warm it was.

So of course Mr Pink-Whistle knew at once

that Mister Mean was the thief. 'The mean, hateful creature!' he said to himself. 'Making an old woman unhappy, just when she had got a little treat ready. Ah, well, Mister Mean, you'll be sorry.'

Mr Pink-Whistle walked up to the door, gave it a loud crack with his fist and flung it open. He stamped in and made a sort of angry growling noise in his throat.

'Who's that?' cried Mister Mean in alarm, for he could see nobody, of course.

Mr Pink-Whistle said nothing. He just made the angry growling noise again. He went to the larder door and threw it open. It was full of goodies! There was a meat pie, a jam tart, a tin of biscuits, two kippers, a large tin of best tea, and some tins of meat. There was a big white loaf of bread in the bin and a pound of butter on a plate.

'Good!' Mr Pink-Whistle growled in his throat. 'Very good! I'll have those!'

He began to take them all off the shelves. Mister Mean, who was shivering in his shoes, jumped up at once. 'Stop thief!' he cried. 'Stop thief! Those are my belongings!'

Mr Pink-Whistle growled again. 'I'm only doing what you've just done this morning!'

he said. 'Where did you get that cake from? Where did you get that blanket? You wicked fellow, to rob an old woman!'

Mister Mean was so terrified to hear a voice and not see anyone that he fell down on his knees and begged for mercy.

'Mercy!' shouted Mr Pink-Whistle, who was now beginning to enjoy himself. 'No! You shan't have any mercy. I might even eat you up!'

'Oh no, don't, don't!' begged Mister Mean, who at once thought that Mr Pink-Whistle must be an invisible giant or something. He didn't know that he was a little man much smaller than he, Mister Mean, was! 'Take all you want – but leave my house and don't come back again. You frighten me! I can't see you! I'll never steal again, never, never, never!'

'Well, see you don't,' said Mr Pink-Whistle, 'or I shall certainly come back and gobble you up in one mouthful!'

Mr Pink-Whistle could hardly keep from giggling when he thought how difficult it would be for him to gobble up Mister Mean. He took the new blanket, and a new rug from the sofa, and set off to Dame Gentle's, carrying as well all the goodies he had found in the larder.

Mother Dilly hadn't yet come back. Dame Gentle had gone into the bedroom to wash her face. There was no one in the kitchen.

Mr Pink-Whistle draped the blanket over one chair and the rug over the other. He put the meat pie, the jam tart, the biscuits, kippers, tea, bread and tins of meat on the table. Then, hearing footsteps, he slipped quietly to one side, and waited.

Dame Gentle came into the kitchen at the same time as Mother Dilly came back. They both saw all the new things at the same time. How they stared! They rubbed their eyes and stared again.

'Do you see what I see?' asked Dame Gentle at last. 'Goodies of all kinds! *And* my blanket and a new rug as well!'

'I see it all!' said Mother Dilly. 'It's very strange – but very pleasant. Let's sit down and eat!'

'Oh, I'm so happy again,' said Dame Gentle. 'Somebody was *very* unkind to me – but now someone else has been even kinder! Blessings on him, whoever he may be! Blessings on his kind head!'

'Thank you,' whispered Mr Pink-Whistle, longing to show himself, but not daring to, in case he frightened the two old ladies. 'Thank you!'

'Funny!' said Dame Gentle, looking all round. 'I thought I heard something. IS ANYBODY HERE?'

But nobody answered. Mr Pink-Whistle had slipped out of the door, and was already on the way to his next adventure. Kind old Pink-Whistle!

Chapter 7

The Two Ugly Creatures

There was once a man that nobody loved. He lived alone in a cottage, and he was angry because he was blind.

He wore black glasses over his two blind eyes, and the children did not like these. So they were afraid of him, and the rudest of them called names after him, which was very unkind of them.

The man had always had weak eyes, but he had been so fond of reading that he had made them worse and worse. Now he couldn't see at all, and he was unhappy and angry. Angry because he knew that if only he had been wise, he would still have been able to see – and unhappy because he wanted to read, and couldn't, and because he had no friends.

People would have liked to be kind to him, but he wouldn't let them. He was bad-tempered, spiteful, and very, very lonely. His face grew uglier and uglier as he frowned more and more, and his black glasses seemed even blacker.

He used to go along the road of the town, tapping with his stick, and muttering to himself as he went, 'It isn't fair. I haven't anything at all! I've no friends. I've no books to read, no pictures to see. It isn't fair!'

And one day, of course, fat little Mr Pink-Whistle met him and heard him. What, something wasn't fair? Ah, Mr Pink-Whistle was all ears when he heard that, you may be sure.

'What isn't fair?' asked Mr Pink-Whistle, falling into step with the blind man.

'Go away,' said the blind man rudely. 'I never talk to anyone. Go away.'

'Then you must be very lonely,' said Mr Pink-Whistle in his gentlest voice.

'What's that to do with you?' said the blind man. 'I'm ugly, I know – even the children call out after me, the little wretches. And I'm bad-tempered. And I'm quite helpless, because I can't see. I often fall off the kerb into the road – but who cares? Nobody at all!'

'You are a very unhappy man,' said Mr Pink-Whistle with a sigh. 'I wish I could find you a friend. All you want is someone to love, and someone who loves *you*.'

The blind man laughed loudly. 'Who would ever love *me*?' he cried. 'If anyone sees me, they run away. I know. I've heard them!'

'Let me help you across the road,' said Mr Pink-Whistle, his heart very sad, for he could not for the life of him think how he might put things right for this poor man.

The blind man at first pushed away Mr Pink-Whistle's hand – and then, because his hand felt so friendly and so kind, he took it after all, and allowed himself to be helped across the road.

'Thanks for helping me,' he said. 'If I could help you in return, maybe I would. But I can't help anyone. I'm just no use at all.'

'You may be sure I'll ask you for help if you can give it,' said Mr Pink-Whistle. 'Goodbye. I'll come and see you again some-time. You live in that small house over there, don't you?'

'Yes,' said the blind man. 'Goodbye.' He went off by himself, tapping with his stick.

Mr Pink-Whistle looked after him. 'It's not fair,' he said. 'Some people have everything – their eyes to see with, good health, friends, love and happiness. And that poor man hasn't anything at all, not even a friend. Yes – it's mostly his own fault, and that only makes it worse!'

The little fat man looked quite sad for once. His eyes lost their twinkle and his mouth drooped. He stood thinking for a moment or two, and then he heard a yelping noise from round the corner. He ran to see what the matter was.

There was a pond round the corner. In it a wet dog struggled for his life. Mr Pink-Whistle waded in and got hold of him. The dog was tied to two big bricks.

'Good gracious!' said Mr Pink-Whistle, cutting the string that bound the dog to the bricks. 'Has someone been trying to drown you?'

'Woof!' said the dog, and as usual Mr Pink-

Whistle understood all he said. 'Yes. The old farmer who lives down the hill sent his man to drown me this morning.'

'How dreadful!' cried Mr Pink-Whistle, trying to dry the dog with his handkerchief. 'Why did he want to do that, little dog?'

'Well, you see,' said the dog sadly. 'I'm so ugly. Look at me and see. My head's too big. My tail is too long. My legs are too short. My ears droop down instead of up. And I'm such an ugly red colour. Everyone laughs at me when they see me, and really, I don't wonder. I saw myself once in a looking-glass outside a shop, and I laughed too.'

'It isn't fair,' said Mr Pink-Whistle, patting the dog. 'You've got a good heart, I am sure, and would be a splendid house-dog. That's all that really matters.'

'Oh, I would, I would!' barked the dog, and he licked Mr Pink-Whistle's hand with a long pink tongue. 'Couldn't you have me for your own? All the other puppies went to good homes, but nobody has ever wanted *me*.'

And then Mr Pink-Whistle had a wonderful idea. 'Listen!' he said. 'I know a poor, ugly, blind man, who is lonely and sad. He wants someone to love him and look after him – someone to sit with him in the evenings, and to guide him when he goes out for walks. He sometimes falls off the kerb, you know. Now do you think your heart is large enough to be this poor man's dog?'

'I would like it better than anything!' yelped the dog. 'But won't he hate me, because I'm ugly?'

'He won't be able to see you,' said Mr Pink-Whistle. 'Come with me now, and we will see what happens.'

So the still-wet dog and the little fat man went to the cottage where the blind man lived. He was there, for he had just come in.

'Hello!' said Mr Pink-Whistle, stepping into the parlour. 'I'm soon back again – and to ask your help too! I've got a poor little dog here, not much more than a puppy, that someone has tried to drown. Could I dry him by the fire, do you think?'

'I'll get a towel,' said the blind man, and he felt his way to a chest, pulled open a drawer and drew out a big brown towel. He went to the hearthrug and knelt down. 'Where's the dog?' he said. 'I used to be fond of dogs, but now even they growl when they see me!'

The wet puppy put out his tongue and gently licked the blind man on the hand. He whined a little. The blind man began to dry him. 'You poor wet creature!' he said. 'So people are unkind to you too, are they? Well, there are two of us, then! Are you hungry? I've got some milk in the larder, and a bone too, I believe. Hey, you, there – would you get them?'

He was calling to Mr Pink-Whistle, but will

you believe it, Mr Pink-Whistle didn't answer a word. No – he just stood by the door, smiling, and the blind man thought he had gone. Mr Pink-Whistle wanted him to do as much as possible for the dog, for he knew that was the right way for them to make friends.

So the man fetched the milk and the bone. He found some biscuits too. He sat down by the fire and listened to the dog eating the food.

And then the puppy-dog jumped on to the man's knees, settled himself comfortably there, and licked the man's hands lovingly. Then he pushed his soft head against the man's face and licked his nose.

'Good dog, good fellow!' said the blind man, and he patted the dog. 'You don't mind how ugly and bad-tempered I am, do you? Well – I won't turn you out just yet. You can stay for a while.'

So the dog stayed. He shared the man's tea with him. He found an old ball and rolled it over the floor. The man heard him playing and smiled for the first time for months. 'See you don't leave it for me to fall over,' he said. So the dog rolled it under the couch when he had finished.

'I don't think I can very well turn you out tonight,' said the blind man, when it was bedtime. 'I will keep you tonight, and when the man who brought you comes back, you shall go then.'

The dog went to sleep on the hearthrug. But in the middle of the night he awoke and heard the blind man tossing and turning. He was always loneliest and unhappiest at night. The dog knew this at once, and he ran to the bed. He jumped up on to the eiderdown and snuggled down beside the man, his nose in the man's hand.

'Good fellow!' said the blind man, patting him. 'Good fellow!'

And do you know, when Mr Pink-Whistle

came that way again, he saw the puppy-dog gambolling round happily, as fat as butter, and the blind man rolling a ball for him which the dog kept fetching and bringing back.

'Hello!' said Mr Pink-Whistle.

'Hello!' cried the blind man. 'You haven't come to fetch the dog have you? I couldn't do without him. You've no idea what a friend he is to me. He loves me and never leaves me for a minute. He guides me when I go out, and he sleeps on my bed at night. He's the finest dog in the world!'

'And my master's the kindest, best man in the world!' yelped the dog. 'He belongs to me. I look after him and make him happy. He doesn't even know I'm ugly!'

'Good!' said Mr Pink-Whistle, looking at the happy face of the blind man, who was no longer ugly and bad-tempered. 'Very good! A little love and friendship go a very long way! Goodbye!'

Chapter 8

The Forgotten Rabbits

In a nice wooden hutch in a lovely garden lived two rabbits. Their names were Bubble and Squeak, and they were very pretty. Their ears were long and floppy, and their noses went up and down all day long.

They belonged to Winnie and Morris. At first the children had been most excited over their rabbits, and had brought them all kinds of delicious food every hour or two. Then they had grown used to them, and had cleaned their cage out and given them food once a day.

And now, lately, they had begun to forget all about them!

For two whole days the hutch had not been cleaned out! For two whole days the rabbits had had no fresh food.

Mother began to wonder if the rabbits were well looked after, and she went down to see. She was very angry when she found that their cage was so dirty and they had no food at all!

'I shall give the rabbits away,' she told Winnie and Morris. 'If you can't look after your own animals, you are not fit to have any.'

'Oh, don't do that,' said Winnie who really liked her rabbits, though she was lazy and couldn't be bothered to remember them. 'I'll clean out the hutch and feed them, really I will, Mummy.'

But she didn't. She remembered for three days, and then she forgot again. And this time her Mummy was away and didn't see that the rabbits were forgotten! Auntie Jane was there to look after the children, and she quite thought that Winnie and Morris could be trusted to see to Bubble and Squeak.

The rabbits were hungry. They gnawed at their cage and tried to get out. They could see the green grass and they could see the cabbages in the kitchen-garden and the nice juicy lettuces. They felt as if they must get to them, somehow.

So they gnawed and they gnawed with their sharp teeth. And after three days, when they were so hungry that they could almost have eaten the wire netting, Bubble made a hole nearly big enough to squeeze through! But not *quite* big enough.

Poor Bubble! He tried to squash his soft body through the hole – and he stuck! He couldn't get forwards and he couldn't get backwards. It was really dreadful.

He began to squeal, and a rabbit squeal is a noise that makes everyone want to rush to its help. There was nobody in the house to hear, because the children and their aunt were out – but Mr Pink-Whistle heard.

He was walking at the end of the street, quite a long way away – but he heard the rabbit squealing, for he had ears that heard all cries of sadness and pain. He stopped and listened. He ran back down the road in a hurry, rushed into the front gate, round the house, and down the garden to where the rabbit hutch was.

He soon saw what had happened to poor Bubble! He carefully cut the hole a little wider, took out the frightened rabbit, and placed it back in the hutch.

'Oh, thank you,' said Bubble, who knew at once that the little fat man was half a brownie.

Mr Pink-Whistle looked rather stern. 'You should not have tried to escape,' he said. 'That was a punishment to you, for trying to run away from a good hutch and kind owners.'

'Please, it isn't a good hutch, and Winnie and Morris are not kind,' said Bubble at once. 'Look – did you ever see such a dirty hutch and nasty hay? Can you see any food at all?'

Mr Pink-Whistle looked – and he frowned.

'No,' he said. 'There is no food at all – and the hutch is very dirty. Are Winnie and Morris unkind to you?'

'Oh yes,' said Squeak, her nose twitching hard, up and down, up and down. 'They often forget us. One day we shall die of hunger – and oh, it's dreadful to be hungry and yet see all that food out there, beyond our cage. That's why we tried to escape.'

'You poor, poor things!' said tender-hearted Mr Pink-Whistle. 'Children have no right to keep pets unless they look after them properly! This is a very wicked thing I hear!'

He opened the door of the cage wide. 'Come out, little rabbits,' he said. 'Go and eat all you want – and then run to the hills and live there in a burrow. I will not let these children keep you.'

The rabbits hopped out gladly. They rushed to the lettuces, which grew in the children's own garden, and they ate the whole lot! They ate a row of new green pea-plants, and they nibbled the tops off the young turnips. Oh, they had a wonderful time! Then off they ran to the hills, and found a cosy burrow for the two of them.

Mr Pink-Whistle stared at the empty cage

and his face was sad. 'What a lot of unfair things happen!' he said. 'Those were harmless, kindly little rabbits – and yet Winnie and Morris made them hungry, thin and miserable! Well, I've put things right for Bubble and Squeak – and now I must see to Winnie and Morris!'

He soon saw the children – bonny, fat and healthy, with rosy faces and shining eyes.

'People don't forget *your* meals!' he thought. 'You are chubby and fat. And *your* beds won't be dirty and smelly, unmade for days! No – they will be sweet and clean and fresh! My dear children, I have to teach you a lesson. You won't like it, but I cannot have you treating little creatures, smaller than yourselves, as unkindly as you have treated those two rabbits.'

Mr Pink-Whistle made himself disappear. He couldn't be seen at all. He went into the house and up the stairs, and soon found the children's rooms with their pretty white beds and blue eiderdowns.

Mr Pink-Whistle pulled all the bedclothes off. He jumped on the white sheets with his dirty boots! What a mess he made of those two nice beds!

'Now the children will know what the rabbits felt like, having no nice clean cage to sleep in!' said Mr Pink-Whistle.

He went downstairs. Aunt Jane had placed two plates of delicious-smelling stew on the table for the children who had gone to wash their hands. Mr Pink-Whistle took the plates and emptied them out of the window! Then he put them back on the table.

What a to-do there was when Aunt Jane and the children came into the dining-room!

'How quickly you've eaten your dinner!' cried Aunt Jane.

'We haven't eaten *any* of it!' said Morris, staring in surprise at his empty plate, smeared with gravy.

'You must have,' said Aunt Jane. 'Your plates are empty. Don't tell naughty stories!'

'We're not!' said Winnie. 'Someone's eaten it instead of us. Can we have some more, Aunt Jane?'

'There isn't any,' said her aunt. 'You must have the pudding now. I simply can't understand it!'

Nor could the children. They were hungry and had so much wanted their stew. Aunt Jane went to get the pudding. It was a treacle pudding, and it sat upright on a big dish. Just as she set the dish on the table and turned round to get a spoon, Mr Pink-Whistle whipped the pudding off the dish and threw it out of the window!

Plonk! It landed on the grass and broke into bits. The children screamed in horror. 'Our pudding! It jumped off the dish!'

Aunt Jane hadn't seen what happened. She was very, very angry. 'You are being naughty children!' she cried. '*You* threw it out of the window – I know you did! It must have been you, for there's no one else here! Look at it there, smashed on the lawn! Go up to bed, both of you!'

Crying bitterly the two children went upstairs to bed – and then they saw their dirty, untidy beds, with the clothes on the floor. They called their aunt, and she looked at the mess in dismay.

'We didn't do it, really we didn't,' sobbed Winnie. 'Please believe us, Aunt Jane.'

Aunt Jane didn't know what to think. She made the beds, and told the children to get undressed. Winnie went to a drawer of her chest as soon as her aunt had gone. 'I've got some biscuits and chocolate here,

Morris,' she said. 'Let's have them. I'm so hungry!'

But as soon as she opened her drawer, Mr Pink-Whistle's invisible hand went in, and he took out the packet of biscuits and the bar of chocolate. He threw them out of the window.

The children screamed with rage and fright. Whatever could be happening! Then Mr Pink-Whistle pulled their beds to pieces again and jumped on the sheets!

'Who is it? Who is it? It's someone we can't see!' wept Winnie.

'Yes,' said Mr Pink-Whistle. 'But now you *shall* see me!' He muttered some very magic words – and hey presto! there he was, standing in front of the children, a little fat man with pointed brownie ears and large green eyes.

'Good morning!' he said. 'I'm sorry to behave like this – but for the sake of Bubble and Squeak I have to put things right. You forgot to clean their bed – so I've made your beds dirty and untidy to show you how horrid it is. You forgot to give them food and they went hungry. So I've taken away your food to show you what it's like to be really hungry. What do you think about it?'

'I'm ashamed,' said Winnie, and she hung her head.

'I'm sorry about it,' said Morris, and he went red. 'I'll go straight down to the hutch now and give the rabbits a good feed.'

Off went the children – and found the hutch empty. How they cried!

'It's a hard lesson,' said Mr Pink-Whistle, feeling sad. 'But learn it, my dears, and you'll be happier in the future – and so will your pets. Goodbye!'

He disappeared. Where had he gone? The children couldn't imagine!

Chapter 9

Jimmy's Day in the Country

It was going to be a very exciting day for fifty of the town children. They were all to go for a day in the country. How lovely!

At ten o'clock a big red bus stood waiting at the corner of the road, and the fifty children climbed in with two grown-ups to look after them. Off they went, singing and laughing.

Each child had his lunch with him and his tea, in school-bags. Jimmy had egg sandwiches, two slices of cake, and and an apple for his lunch; and jam sandwiches, two buns, and a piece of chocolate for his tea. He thought it was lovely.

'Now, listen,' said Miss White, one of the grown-ups, when at last the bus arrived at a farm in the country. 'You may all wander off as you please, and see all the animals on the farm – but be sure not to go out of reach of the bell, because the bus will take us back at five o'clock, and you must all be here then. I shall ring the bell at half-past four to warn you.'

The children ran off, talking happily. Some went to see the pretty new calves. Some ran to see the ducks and the hens. Others begged for a ride on the old brown horse, and Jimmy waited for his turn too. He had been in the country before and he loved it.

Very soon he felt hungry, and he found a sunny place beneath a hedge and sat down to eat his lunch. Oooh! How good the egg sandwiches were! The cake was delicious, and the apple was as sweet as sugar.

'I mustn't eat my tea as well now, though I'd very much like to!' said Jimmy, looking at his jam sandwiches. 'No – I'll leave them till four o'clock.'

He packed up his bag again, put it over his shoulder, and went off across the fields to see if he could find some flowers to take home to his mother.

He knew his way about very well, for he had been down to the farm before. He jumped over a little stream, crossed two fields, and went into a wood. Big pink flowers were growing there, and Jimmy began to make a bunch of them. He went right through the wood, and came out at the other side. There was a field that used to have goats in.

'I wonder if the goats have any babies,' thought Jimmy to himself. 'I love little kid-goats!'

He went to see – and there, under the hedge, he saw a small girl, with tears rolling down her cheeks. She belonged to Jimmy's party, and he looked at her in surprise.

'Whatever's the matter?' he asked.

'It's those horrid goats,' sobbed the small girl, whose name was Margery. 'I came here, and lay down in the sunshine, and somehow I fell asleep. And two big goats came whilst I was asleep and ate all my lunch – yes, and my tea too. And they even ate my bag as well! This is all that's left of it – look!'

She showed him the strap. Jimmy was sorry for her. 'It must be dreadful to have your lunch and your tea both eaten by goats,' he thought.

'Have you eaten your lunch?' asked Margery, looking at his bag hungrily. 'I suppose you couldn't share it with me?'

'I've eaten it,' said Jimmy. And then, because he was a kind boy, he said, 'But you can have my tea if you like! My mother will give me some more when I get home!'

'Oh, thank you!' said Margery – and she ate up every scrap of Jimmy's nice tea – chocolate and all!

'Now I'll take you where there are wild strawberries,' she said. 'I found them last year in the wood.'

But although they hunted for ages and ages they couldn't find any at all. 'It's time for the bell soon, I should think,' said Jimmy. 'Don't let's go too far.'

When the bell rang at half-past four, Jimmy was dreadfully hungry – but his tea was inside Margery! So he couldn't have any! 'Come along,' he said. 'We must go back. The bus will be there.'

So back they went – but Margery was tired and couldn't hurry. And then she fell down and hurt her knee so badly that she howled and howled! Jimmy bathed her knee in some water and tied it up with his handkerchief. Then he tried to hurry Margery along, but she could only limp very slowly, for her knee hurt her.

'We shall miss the bus!' cried Jimmy in despair. 'Do hurry!'

Margery cried. She fell over again. Jimmy knelt down and made her get on his back. 'I'll give you a piggyback,' he said. 'Maybe we'll be quicker then.'

But Margery was heavy and he couldn't carry her for long. 'Let's sit down here and wait for the bus to go by,' said Margery at last. 'We can stop it then.'

So they sat down – but, alas, for them! the bus went another way, and they saw it turning a corner far down the hill, full of children going home!

'Oh, it's too bad!' cried Jimmy, almost in tears. 'I've helped you all I could, Margery, and given you my tea and carried you – and now we've missed the bus and my mother will be worried.'

'Look – here's someone coming,' said Margery. They looked down the lane, and saw a fat little man. It was Mr Pink-Whistle, of course, and he was going home for a little holiday. He had been away from his cottage and his cat, Sooty, for quite a long while.

He saw the children and stopped. 'What's the matter?' he asked.

Margery told him all their story. 'It's too bad for poor Jimmy,' she said. 'He did help me such a lot, and he was so kind – and now I've made him miss the bus and we haven't any money and we've got to walk home, and my knee hurts, and . . .'

'Good gracious me!' said Mr Pink-Whistle. 'How very lucky that I happened to walk down this way. I'll soon put things right! That's what I'm made for, I think – to put things right. But you wouldn't believe what a lot of things go wrong! I'm always hard at work, every single day.'

'I like you,' said Margery, and she put her small hand into Mr Pink-Whistle's rather large one. 'You look a bit like a brownie in my picture book at home. But how can you put things right for us? There isn't another bus home.'

'Oh yes, there is,' said Mr Pink-Whistle. 'It's not the usual bus, you know – it's one that nobody sees but the little folk of the woods! But if you'd really like to see it, just put on these glasses, will you? They will help you.'

He handed the two surprised children a pair of glasses each. They set them on their noses and looked through them.

My goodness! What a marvellous surprise! They could see small brownies peeping at them from the hedge. They could see tiny folk of all sorts running here and there, no bigger than flowers. And they could see a strange little cottage standing not far off, which they were quite certain hadn't been there before!

'It *was* there before,' said Mr Pink-Whistle, 'but you hadn't got those magic glasses on, so you just didn't see it! A friend of mine lives there. Let's see if she will give us tea.'

They went up to the little green door. Rat-tat! The door opened and a small woman stood there, with big pointed ears just like Mr Pink-Whistle's. Her eyes were green too, like his. She beamed all over her face and cried, 'Mr Pink-Whistle! What a lovely surprise! You're just in time for tea. Do come in!'

So they all went in, and Mr Pink-Whistle told his friend, Dame Little, all about Jimmy and Margery. They sat down to tea – and, my goodness, what a tea it was! There were wild strawberries and cream. There were little biscuits shaped like flowers. There were cakes shaped like animals, and they were full of cream. The funny part about them was that when you pressed them, each cake squeaked! But Jimmy didn't squeeze too hard, because it shot the cream out! What a tea it was!

'The bus will be by soon,' said Dame Little. So they shook hands with her, and she took them to her gate. Down the lane came

the bus – but what a bus! It was shaped like a Noah's ark on wheels, and you had to climb up a ladder and get in at the lid, which the conductor held open!

Inside there were rows of seats, and on them sat rabbits, moles, a hedgehog, brownies, and many other passengers. They looked rather surprised to see the children, but made room for them most politely. The strange bus started off and the conductor shut the lid.

'This is a most surprising adventure,' said Jimmy. 'I can't believe it's true.'

'Well, you don't need to believe, it,' said Mr Pink-Whistle, laughing. 'Think it's a dream, if you like – it will be just as exciting, either way!'

The bus stopped at the end of the children's street, and they got out, yawning. 'Thank you very much, Mr Pink-Whistle,' began Jimmy, but Mr Pink-Whistle was gone – and so was the bus.

'*Was* it a dream, do you think?' said Margery to Jimmy. 'I wish I knew!'

'Well, all I can say is that I'm jolly glad I helped you, Margery,' said Jimmy. 'I'd never have had this lovely adventure if I hadn't!'

Chapter 10

The Mean Little Boy

There was once a mean little boy called Wilfrid. He took other children's toys away and wouldn't give them back. He pinched the little girls when no grown-up was about. He hit the little boys, and sometimes threw their caps right up into the trees so that they couldn't get them.

Wilfrid was big and rather strong for his age, and it wasn't much good trying to stop him. All that the other children could do was to run away when they saw him.

But one day little Janet didn't run away quickly enough. She was playing with her tricycle in the street and Wilfrid saw her. He loved riding on tricycles because he hadn't got one himself – so up he ran and caught hold of the handle.

'Get off, Janet. I want a ride,' said Wilfrid.

'No,' said Janet. 'You are much bigger than I am, and my mother says I mustn't let bigger children ride my little tricycle in case they break it.'

'Well, I'm jolly well going to ride it!' said Wilfrid. He dragged Janet off her tricycle and she fell on the ground. Wilfrid was always so rough. Then he got on the little tricycle himself and rode off quickly down the street, ringing the bell loudly.

My word, how quickly he went! You should have seen him. All the other children skipped out of the way, and even the grown-ups did, too. Ting-a-ling-a-ling! went the bell – ting-a-ling-a-ling!

Wilfrid came to where the street began to go down a little hill. On he went, just as fast – and then he came to a roadway. He tried to stop, but he couldn't. Over the kerb he went, crash! The tricycle fell over, and Wilfrid fell too.

He didn't hurt himself – but the tricycle was quite broken! The handle was off, the bell was spoilt and wouldn't ring, and one of the pedals was broken!

A little fat man with pointed ears and green eyes saw the accident. It was Mr Pink-Whistle of course, trotting along as usual to see what bad things in the world he could put right.

He hurried up to the boy who had fallen, meaning to pick him up and comfort him, but before he could get there a little girl ran up and began to scold him, crying bitterly all the time.

'You horrid boy, Wilfrid! Now you've broken my tricycle and I did love it so much.

My mother will be very angry with me because you rode it. I shan't be able to get it mended, and it will have to be put away in the shed and never ridden any more!'

And Janet cried bucketfuls of tears all down herself till her dress was quite damp. The other children came running up to see what had happened. They glared at Wilfrid, who made a face and slapped Janet because she cried so loudly.

'It's a silly tricycle anyway!' said Wilfrid. 'Stupid baby one. Good gracious, I might have broken my leg, falling over like that!'

He stalked off, whistling, leaving the others to pick up the tricycle and to comfort poor Janet.

'Horrid boy!' said Tom. 'Don't cry, Janet.'

'Yes, but it isn't fair!' wept Janet. 'It's *my* tricycle, and he took it away from me – and now it's broken and my mother will be so cross.'

Mr Pink-Whistle was sorry for the little girl. He walked up to the children and patted Janet's golden head.

'Now, now, don't cry any more,' he said. 'Maybe *I* can mend your tricycle. Tell me some more about the boy who broke it.'

Well, you should have heard the things that came pouring out about Wilfrid, the mean boy! Mr Pink-Whistle didn't care whether it was telling tales or not – he just *had* to know about him. And soon he knew so much that a big frown came above his green eyes and he pursed up his pink mouth.

'Hmmmm,' said Mr Pink-Whistle, deep down in his throat. 'I must see into this. That boy wants punishing. But first we will mend your tricycle, little girl.'

Well, Mr Pink-Whistle took the broken tricycle along to a bicycle shop, and soon it was as good as new. The handle was put on again very firmly. A new bell was bought and fixed on. It was much better than the other one. The pedal was nicely mended – and then Janet got on her tricycle and rode off in delight.

'Oh, thank you!' she cried. 'But I do hope I don't meet Wilfrid! He will want to ride my tricycle again and break it!'

'I'll look after Wilfrid!' said Mr Pink-Whistle. And then, in his very sudden and extraordinary way, he disappeared! One minute he was there – and the next he wasn't. But really and truly he *was* there –

but quite invisible, because, as you know, he was half magic.

He had seen Wilfrid coming along again – and Mr Pink-Whistle meant to watch that small boy and see all the things he did! Yes – Wilfrid wasn't going to have a very good time now.

Wilfrid strolled along, hands in pockets, making faces at children he met. When he met Kenneth, who was eating a rosy apple, Wilfrid stopped.

'Give me that apple!' he said.

'No!' said Kenneth, putting the apple behind his back. Wilfrid snatched at it – and it rolled into the mud so that nobody could eat it at all!

Kenneth yelled. Wilfrid grinned. Mr Pink-Whistle frowned. The little fat man bought another apple at the fruit-shop and slipped it into Kenneth's pocket without being seen. He would find it there when he got home – what a lovely surprise!

Then Mr Pink-Whistle suddenly became visible again, and walked into a shop. He bought several rather large sheets of white paper, some pins, and some black chalk. He stood by a wall and quickly wrote something in big letters on a sheet of paper.

Then he disappeared suddenly – but a very strange thing happened. On Wilfrid's back a large sheet of white paper suddenly appeared, and was gently pinned there so that Wilfrid didn't know. On the paper was written a single sentence in big black letters: 'I KNOCKED KENNETH'S APPLE INTO THE MUD!'

Well, Wilfrid went along the street humming gaily, not knowing that anything was on his back at all. But very soon all the children knew it. First one saw it, then another – and soon a big crowd was following Wilfrid, giggling hard.

Wilfrid heard them and turned round.

'What's the joke?' he asked.

'*You're* the joke!' said Harry.

'You stop giggling and tell me *how* I'm the joke!' said Wilfrid fiercely.

'Who knocked Kenneth's apple into the mud?' called Jenny.

'How do you know I did?' cried Wilfrid. 'I suppose that baby Kenneth has been telling tales. Wait till I see him again!'

'No he hasn't told us – you told us yourself, giggled Doris.

'I didn't,' said Wilfrid.

'Look on your back!' shouted Lennie.

Wilfrid screwed his head and looked over his shoulder. He caught sight of something white on his back. He dragged at his coat and pulled off the paper. He read it and went red with rage.

'Who dared to pin this on my back!' he shouted. 'I'll shake him till his teeth rattle!'

Everyone shook their heads. No – they hadn't pinned the paper on Wilfrid's back, though they would have liked to, if they had dared.

Wilfrid threw the paper on to the ground and stamped on it. 'If anyone does that to me again, they'll be sorry for themselves!' he said fiercely. 'So just look out!'

But the one who had done it didn't care a rap for Wilfrid's threat. No – old Pink-Whistle grinned to himself and trotted quietly along after Wilfrid, waiting to see what mean thing the boy would do next.

And then out would come another sheet of paper, of course – and Wilfrid would have to wear another notice on his back.

Chapter 11

Wilfrid Has a
Good Many Shocks

Mr Pink-Whistle followed Wilfrid home, and then he sat on the wall outside, still invisible, to wait for him to come out. Inside the house he could hear Wilfrid being very rude to his mother.

'Wilfrid, I want you to run down and get me some potatoes,' said his mother.

'I don't want to, I'm tired,' said the selfish boy.

'Now you do as you're told, Wilfrid,' said his mother. 'Hurry up.'

'Shan't!' said Wilfrid. 'I'm tired, I tell you.'

Mr Pink-Whistle listened, quite horrified. To think that any boy could talk to his mother like that! It was simply dreadful. Wilfrid went on being rude – and then, when his mother had gone to the back door to speak to the baker, Wilfrid slipped out of the front door. *He* wasn't going to go and fetch potatoes, not he!

Mr Pink-Whistle had been busy writing something on a sheet of white paper with his black chalk. He waited till Wilfrid passed him, and then the little fat man neatly pinned the paper on to Wilfrid's back. He did it with such a magic touch that the boy didn't feel anything at all. Off went Wilfrid down the street, whistling – and on his back the sheet of paper said: 'I HAVE BEEN VERY RUDE TO MY MOTHER!'

Well, it wasn't long before all the passers-by saw the paper and began to laugh at it. 'Fancy!' they said to one another, 'he has been rude to his mother! Well, he certainly looks a most unpleasant boy, it's true – but fancy being rude to his *mother*!'

The other children soon saw the notice and gathered round, giggling. Wilfrid glared at them. Whatever was all the giggling about?

'You've been rude to your mother!' shouted Kenneth.

'Bad boy! You've been rude to your mother!' yelled all the children.

Wilfrid stopped in surprise. Now how in the world did the others know that? He hadn't told anyone – and his mother certainly hadn't, for she would be too much ashamed of her son to say such a thing.

'How do you know?' he demanded angrily.

'You've got it on your back,' shouted the children in glee.

Wilfrid tore the paper off his back and looked at it. How he scowled when he saw what was printed there! But how could it have got on his back? And who could have written that sentence?

He tore the paper into little pieces and stuffed them into a litter bin. Then he stamped off angrily. Just wait till he caught anyone pinning paper on his back again! He kept turning round quickly to make sure that no one was creeping behind him.

Soon he met Alison, and she had a bag of sweets. 'Give me one!' said Wilfrid.

'No,' said Alison bravely. Wilfrid gave her such a pinch that she squealed loudly and ran away, hugging her bag of sweets and crying.

Well, you can guess that it wasn't more than half a minute before Mr Pink-Whistle had pinned another sheet of paper on

Wilfrid's back! This time it said, in bold black letters: 'I HAVE PINCHED ALISON AND MADE HER CRY.'

Everyone who saw it looked surprised – and then grinned. 'What a nasty little boy that must be!' they thought. They wondered if he knew that he had the paper on his back. He didn't know at first – but as soon as he met some other children, he knew at once!

For they danced around him, shouting, 'You pinched Alison! You horrid boy! You pinched Alison and made her cry!'

'How do you know?' shouted Wilfrid. 'Did she tell tales of me?'

'No – you're telling tales about yourself!' yelled back the children, keeping a good distance away from the angry little boy. He at once felt round at his back and tore off the paper. When he read what was written he was rather frightened. He felt quite certain that no one had been near enough to him to pin on that paper – he had been keeping a good watch. Then how did it get on his back?

Wilfrid thought he would go home. He didn't like these strange happenings at all. It wasn't a bit funny suddenly to have horrid things pinned on his back for people to laugh at. He ran home quickly.

His mother was out in the garden. Wilfrid thought that no one else was in the house, so he crept to the jam cupboard, and looked for a pot of strawberry jam. He didn't know that Mr Pink-Whistle was just behind him, quite invisible! The naughty boy ran off with the jam and sat down under a bush in the front garden to enjoy it.

Mr Pink-Whistle busily wrote on another sheet of paper, then sat down beside Wilfrid, and pinned it gently on his back. The boy couldn't see Mr Pink-Whistle, of course, and he was so busy with the jam that he didn't even hear the very slight rustle of the paper.

He finished the jam and went indoors, and as soon as he turned round his mother saw what was pinned on his back: 'I HAVE STOLEN A POT OF STRAWBERRY JAM.'

'Oh, *have* you!' said Wilfrid's mother, and she went to her jam cupboard to look. Sure enough a pot was gone.

'Wilfrid! You bad boy! You've taken my jam!' she cried. 'Go straight upstairs to bed and stay there for the rest of the day! Go quickly before I scold you some more!'

Wilfrid rushed upstairs, for his mother was really very angry indeed. He took his coat off to undress – and saw the notice that said so plainly, 'I HAVE STOLEN A POT OF STRAWBERRY JAM.'

Wilfrid stared at it, frightened. Who had seen him take the jam? Who had pinned that notice on him? It was magic. It couldn't be anything else. Wilfrid began to cry.

'Oh, it's all very well to cry,' said the voice of Mr Pink-Whistle in the bedroom. 'You cry just because you are frightened – not because you are sorry. You are a very horrid, rude and mean little boy.'

'Oh, who's speaking to me?' asked Wilfrid, staring all round the room and seeing nobody. 'I'm so frightened. Please, please, don't pin any more notices on me. I can't bear it.'

'I shall go on pinning notices on you just as long as you do things that deserve it,' said Mr Pink-Whistle. 'I say again – you are a very horrid, rude and mean little boy.'

There was a silence. Mr Pink-Whistle had gone. Wilfrid slowly got undressed and climbed into bed. He lay there with nothing to do, thinking very hard.

Yes – the strange voice was right. He was a horrid boy. He had spoilt Kenneth's apple – broken Janet's tricycle – been rude to his mother – stolen her pot of jam – pinched Alison – good gracious, what a long list of horridness!

'If only I could put things right!' thought Wilfrid uncomfortably. 'It's so easy to do something wrong – and so difficult to put it right afterwards.'

His mother came into the room, very angry. Wilfrid called to her, 'Mother! I'm sorry I was rude today – and please forgive me for taking the jam. I never will again. Can I take some money out of my money-box and buy another pot for you?'

'Well – that would be very nice of you and would put everything right again, Wilfrid,' said his mother, surprised and pleased. 'You can get up and go and buy it now, before you change your mind.'

'I shan't change my mind,' said Wilfrid, and he hurriedly dressed again. He had been saving up to buy a big bow and some arrows – but never mind! He tipped all the money out of his box. There was eight pounds and thirty pence. He put it all into his pocket.

He rushed out. He went to the grocer's and bought a large pot of best strawberry jam. He went to the greengrocer's and bought two apples for Kenneth. He went to the toy shop and bought a doll for Alison, and a tricycle basket for Janet. All his money was spent!

The other children were most astonished when they saw Wilfrid coming along looking ashamed and shy! He was always so bold and rude!

'Kenneth – here's something for you,' said Wilfrid, and he pushed the apples into the boy's hands. 'Alison – I didn't mean to hurt you and make you cry. Here's a doll to make up for it. And, Janet – here's a new basket to put on the front of your tricycle. I'm sorry I broke it.'

'Oh, Wilfrid!' cried all three children in the greatest delight. 'How nice of you! Thank you very much.'

Wilfrid went red and ran home with the jam. He gave it to his mother and she kissed him.

'There's nobody can be nicer than you when you really try!' she said.

'Really, Mother?' said Wilfrid, feeling very happy all of a sudden. 'Oh, Mother – I don't know how those horrid notices came on my back, but I do hope there won't be any more, now I've tried to put things right!'

Well – there was one more! Mr Pink-Whistle had watched Wilfrid trying to put things right, and he was pleased. He followed the boy about for a few more days and saw that he really was trying to be better. So he put one more notice on Wilfrid's back – and then went off to another town to see if he could find something else to put right.

What was on that last paper? Something that Wilfrid didn't mind at all! It said: 'I REALLY HAVE BEEN DOING MY BEST!'

And all the children clapped their hands and cried, 'Yes, Wilfrid – you have!"

Mr Pink-Whistle Interferes

Mr Pink-Whistle Interferes

Enid Blyton

Illustrations by Kevin Kimber

BLOOMSBURY
CHILDREN'S
BOOKS

Contents

1 Mr Pink-Whistle Interferes   135
2 A Wonderful Party   152
3 A Puzzle for the Jones Family   167
4 Mr Pink-Whistle's Circus   179
5 Mr Pink-Whistle and the Cowards   189
6 Mr Pink-Whistle and the Money-Box   201
7 Mr Pink-Whistle Has a Good Idea   213
8 Mr Pink-Whistle and the Eggs   226

Chapter 1

Mr Pink-Whistle Interferes

I hope you remember dear old Pink-Whistle, the little man who is half a brownie, and has pointed ears? He can make himself invisible if he wants to, and he goes about the world trying to put wrong things right.

One day Mr Pink-Whistle walked into the village of Little-Trees. There was a market there, and he wanted to buy some fish for Sooty, his cat. In the middle of the market were three stalls, and one man and his wife ran all of them.

One was for groceries, one was for fruit and vegetables, and the third one was for fish. Mr Pink-Whistle looked at the man who was serving at the fish stall, and he didn't much like what he saw.

'What a nasty-looking fellow!' thought Pink-Whistle. 'What a toothy smile – and what horrid, little eyes, set so close together that they're almost touching! And his wife isn't much better.'

He didn't think he wanted to go and buy anything from the fish stall, but it seemed to be the only one there. So he went up to buy.

'Who's the man who runs these stalls?' he asked an old woman next to him.

'It's Tom Twisty and his wife,' said the old woman. 'Like name, like nature, I say! We never seem to get our proper weight of goods, or the right amount. But everyone's afraid of Tom Twisty. He owns half the houses in our village, and once he turned one of us out because we dared to complain about his goods.'

Mr Pink-Whistle watched Tom Twisty carefully. He was counting out some oranges for a little girl. 'Let me see, you want twenty. Hold out your basket. That's right. Now – one, two, three – oh, that nearly rolled out, didn't it? Five, six, seven – wait a bit, that's a bad one – oh, no, it isn't – nine, ten, eleven, twelve – how's your mother today, dear? Better, I hope. Fifteen, sixteen, seventeen –

will there be enough room in the basket? Ah, yes – nineteen, twenty!'

Well, I don't know if you have managed to see how Tom Twisty cheated the little girl out of five oranges, but he certainly did. If you read his little speech again, you will soon find out! She paid him for twenty oranges and went off with only fifteen in her basket!

Mr Pink-Whistle was smart, and he saw at once that Tom Twisty had cheated the little girl. He stood still and watched, getting very angry indeed.

He saw Tom Twisty weigh out two pounds of flour, but Mr Pink-Whistle was quite sure there were *not* two pounds there. He saw him empty eight pounds of potatoes into somebody's basket – but quite a pound of dirt went in with them too, and was paid for as potatoes. Dear, dear, dear – what a rogue Twisty was, to be sure!

Mr Pink-Whistle went up for his fish. He asked for two pounds, and Tom Twisty's wife served him. She was not all smiles like her husband – she was a sulky-looking woman. She slapped the fish down in her scales, and although Mr Pink-Whistle was sure that it did not weigh two pounds, down tipped the fish to one side, balancing the pound weights the other side.

'Is that really *two* pounds?' said Pink-Whistle. The woman glared at him.

'How dare you say I'm cheating you!' she cried in a shrill voice.

'I'm not saying that you are,' said Pink-Whistle, in a mild sort of voice. 'I just asked you if that was really *two* pounds? I want to know.'

Mrs Twisty picked up the fish and threw it straight at Mr Pink-Whistle. It knocked his hat off. He picked up the fish, wrapped it in a bit of paper, paid for it, raised his hat, and went off without a word. Mrs Twisty stared after him.

'I'll get the policeman here next time you come!' she yelled after him. 'That I will. Accusing honest people of cheating! Ho, you wait till next time!'

Mr Pink-Whistle slipped into a shop. The shopkeeper was a friend of his and nodded to him. 'May I use your scales for a moment?' asked Pink-Whistle politely, and popped his packet of fish on the scales there. He put a two-pound weight on the other side. Down it went, and Mr Pink-Whistle stared solemnly.

'That fish can only weigh about a pound and a half,' he said. 'Yet I saw that it went down on the scales with a bump when it was weighed before – and I paid for two pounds.'

'You've been to old Twisty's stalls!' said his friend. 'He's a bad lot, and so is his wife. Cheating all the time. But he's rich and powerful and people are afraid to complain. They say he is friendly with the policeman too – pays him to keep away from the market when he's there with his stalls.'

'Hum!' said Mr Pink-Whistle. 'Well, well!

What a shame to cheat all the little girls and old women and busy housewives. I've a good mind to put this right.'

'Don't you meddle with Twisty,' said his friend. 'He'll get the better of you. He's as sharp as a bagful of monkeys.'

'Well, maybe I'm as sharp as *two* bags full,' said Pink-Whistle, with one of his big grins. 'Thank you for the use of your scales, friend. Goodbye.'

Now Mr Pink-Whistle was quite determined to look very closely at the scales and the weights on Tom Twisty's stall, so he went back in the dinner-hour and waited for Twisty and his wife to leave for a meal.

But they didn't. They sat and ate their dinner close by their stalls. Still, that didn't worry Pink-Whistle much. He decided to make himself invisible and do a little examining of the scales without being seen.

In a trice the little man had disappeared. He was quite invisible! He walked over to the three stalls and began to examine a pair of scales. He tipped them up, and saw that something was stuck to the underside of the scale into which the goods were tipped for weighing.

'Aha!' said Pink-Whistle to himself. 'Oho! So this is another little trick – to stick something heavy under the scale-pan to make goods weigh more than they do! That is how my one and a half pounds of fish seemed to weigh *two* pounds. What horrid cheats!'

Tom Twisty and his wife heard the scales rattling a little and they looked up, wondering if anyone was meddling with them. But there was no one to be seen. Pink-Whistle was quite invisible, of course.

'Funny,' said Twisty to his wife. 'I quite thought I saw that scale-pan move.'

'Nonsense,' said his wife.

Pink-Whistle then took up the weights, and weighed them carefully in his hands. They seemed unusually light to him. Perhaps the Twistys used weights that were too light – so that they did not have to give so many apples, or so much sugar or butter! The cheats!

He took the weights over to another stall, belonging to a man called Bill Bonny. Bill had gone off to his dinner. Pink-Whistle popped one of Bill's pound weights into one side of the scales there, and put Twisty's into the other side. Down went Bill's weight with a bang, and up went Twisty's!

'Oho! So it's what I thought. Twisty is using weights that are much too light. His pound weight is not a pound weight and his half-pound weight only weighs about six ounces instead of eight. The rogue! He must have cheated scores of people all the time he has been here!'

He put back the weights beside Twisty's scales. Twisty heard a little noise and looked up, puzzled. But there was nothing to see, of course. Pink-Whistle looked into the sacks of potatoes. All of them had plenty of dirt as well as potatoes! Every little nasty trick that could be used to cheat people out of their goods was here.

'Time this was put right,' said Pink-Whistle to himself. 'High time! And I'll put it right too. I'll stand by Twisty's stall this afternoon and give him a shock!'

So that afternoon, when people came to the market once more to buy, Mr Pink-Whistle was standing close to Twisty at his stall. But nobody could see Pink-Whistle. He was still invisible! He was grinning to himself, because he knew he was going to have a good time. So was everyone, except Twisty and his wife.

A little boy came up with a bag. 'Twelve grapefruit, please,' he said.

Twisty beamed all over his nasty face. He took up a grapefruit and tossed it into the bag. 'One – two – three – I say, that was a fine big one, wasn't it – I'll choose you another fat one – here it is – five – and another, six –'

'Hey, you can't count!' boomed a voice right in Twisty's ear, making him jump violently. He wondered which of the crowd round him was shouting like that, and was quite prepared to throw something at him. But he couldn't see anyone shouting.

'Count your grapefruit, sonny,' boomed Mr Pink-Whistle, making Twisty jump again. 'Have you got six?'

'No, five,' said the little boy.

'Story-teller. I gave you six!' shouted Twisty.

'You gave him five!' yelled Pink-Whistle, putting his mouth close to Twisty's ear. 'Begin again! and *I'll* count this time!'

Twisty was scared. He looked round for the man with the fierce voice, but he couldn't see him at all. The little boy tossed the grapefruit on to the stall, grinning. Twisty, looking rather alarmed, began to count again.

'One, two, three!' – but a voice boomed in his ear.

'*I'M* COUNTING THIS TIME!' And then the voice went on, as Twisty threw the grapefruit one by one into the boy's bag. 'One, two, three – isn't it a lovely day – three, four, five – you're a nice little boy, you are! Four, five, six, seven – that was a nice fat one, wasn't it? – seven, eight, nine, ten – did you say you wanted twelve? Ah, yes, nine, ten, eleven, twelve!'

Of course, you can quite well see that dear old Pink-Whistle was playing Twisty's trick the other way round, giving the little boy far more grapefruit than he asked for, instead of less! Everyone began to shriek with laughter. Twisty was too frightened to say anything, and he meekly let the little boy pay him for twelve grapefruit, when he really had eighteen.

'But I've got eighteen gr –' began the little boy in surprise.

'That's all right,' said Mr Pink-Whistle's voice, in Twisty's ear. 'Twisty's pleased about that, aren't you, Twisty?'

Twisty wasn't. But he didn't dare to say so. Then someone went to Mrs Twisty's stall, and asked for twelve pounds of potatoes. Pink-Whistle popped over to her at once.

He watched the masses of dirt going into the scales with the potatoes. Before Mrs Twisty knew what was happening, Pink-Whistle had tipped up the sack and emptied quite half a dozen more pounds into the scales.

'Sorry there's so much dirt,' said Pink-Whistle's booming voice, right in Mrs Twisty's ear. 'You shall have a few extra pounds of potatoes instead. Can't bear to cheat anyone, you know!'

Mrs Twisty jumped. Where *did* that voice come from? And how did the potato sack suddenly tip itself up like that and empty more potatoes into the scales? She began to tremble. All the same, she wasn't going to let so many potatoes go! She picked out about six.

A sharp slap made her drop them into the pan. 'Naughty, naughty!' said the voice. 'Put a few more in for that.'

And to Mrs Twisty's horror, the sack of potatoes appeared to lift itself up and empty another score or so of potatoes into the big scale-pan!

Who had slapped her? She glared round at everyone, but there did not seem to be anyone near enough. All the people were laughing. What a joke! They didn't quite know what was happening, and most of them were feeling very puzzled, but all the same, how they were enjoying themselves! The Twistys were cheats – and now, for the first time, they were being punished well and truly in full view of the market! *What* a joke!

Mrs Twisty said no more about potatoes. She turned away and pretended to be busy. Somebody went up to buy a pound of flour from Twisty. He slapped his pound weight on one side of the scale, and emptied flour into the other.

'*That's* not a pound!' said the Voice, from somewhere near his ear. 'Here, put *this* weight on – it really does weigh a pound!'

And, to Twisty's horror, a pound weight was put into his scales, and his own weighed against it. Everyone cried out in scorn.

'Huh! Look at that! Twisty's weight has gone up and the other has gone down! Twisty's doesn't weigh a pound!'

Twisty began to shake at the knees. 'Good people, it's a mistake,' he stammered. 'There's some trickery going on here –'

'There certainly is,' said the Voice, 'and there has been trickery going on for a long time! Good people, tell Twisty to turn up his scale-pans! See what is underneath!'

Twisty tried to look fierce. He looked round for the man with the voice. Where *could* he be? 'I'll slap your face hard!' cried Twisty, bravely.

'Go on, then!' mocked Pink-Whistle, and poked Twisty in the chest. 'Slap me! Here I am!'

Twisty was terrified. He couldn't bear being punched by someone who wasn't there. The people roared at him.

'Lift up your scale-pans, Mr and Mrs Twisty! Lift up your scale-pans, and let us see underneath!'

Pink-Whistle lifted them up himself, and there, stuck underneath the pans into which goods were put to be weighed, were lumps of clay, flattened on to the pans to make them weigh more than they should.

Then the people went quite mad. They made for the sacks of potatoes and apples, they went for the sacks of flour and bags of pepper, they rushed at the slabs of fish – and before the two bad Twistys knew what was happening, they were being pelted with potatoes, apples, and fish, and having flour and pepper emptied all over them!

'You'll be sorry for this,' sobbed Mrs Twisty. 'I'll turn you all out of your houses!'

'WHAT'S THAT?' boomed the Voice that the Twistys now feared more than anything. 'Say that again!'

'No, no!' said Twisty, scared to death. 'She didn't mean it. We're both sorry for all the wrong things we've done. People can help themselves to any of our market goods they please today!'

'And will you behave yourselves in future?' boomed the Voice.

'Yes, yes,' said Twisty. 'Certainly. No doubt about that.'

The Twistys left the market in a hurry, and went home. The people helped themselves to all the goods on the stalls, laughing and chattering. Pink-Whistle laughed too, then made himself visible again and went after the Twistys.

When he got to their house he saw them coming out with their bags. They were off and away! They were too scared to stay in the village of Little-Trees any longer. They caught the first bus that came along, and Mr Pink-Whistle got in with them. The bus would soon pass his own house, so that was very convenient for him.

The Twistys saw the little man opposite them and heard him humming a little tune. Mrs Twisty suddenly noticed his pointed ears, and she nudged her husband.

'Look! That man's half a brownie. Look at his ears. Oh, Twisty – do you think he had anything to do with that upset at the market?'

Pink-Whistle saw them looking at him, and he grinned. Aha! The Twistys wouldn't play such tricks any more! They would be very, very careful in future.

He took out his packet of fish and sniffed at it. Then he looked at Twisty. 'I bought this at the market today,' he said, 'and do you know, though it only weighs a pound and a half, the person who sold it to me said it weighed two pounds. And . . .'

But the Twistys had leapt out of the bus and gone. They had recognised that Voice. Oooooh! They were too scared to ride in the bus any longer. Where they went to nobody knows, and certainly nobody cares.

Pink-Whistle chuckled. 'Another thing put right!' he said. 'Won't old Sooty laugh when she hears *this* tale!'

And Sooty certainly did!

Chapter 2

A Wonderful Party

Now one day Mr Pink-Whistle met such a nice pair of children that he really had to stop and talk to them. The girl had a bright, smiling face, and the boy looked so friendly and had such twinkling eyes that Mr Pink-Whistle couldn't help smiling when he saw him.

'Hello, hello there!' said Mr Pink-Whistle, looking at the two children. 'Are you twins? You look exactly alike!'

'Yes, we're twins,' said the boy. 'We were born on the same day. Mollie will be eight on Thursday and so shall I.'

'Ha! A birthday!' said Mr Pink-Whistle, who loved presents and surprises. 'I suppose you will be having a party?'

'Oh, of course,' said Mollie. 'Michael has chosen six boys and I have chosen six girls – so it will be a lovely big party; and do you know what Mike and I are going to have – a lucky dip! You see, Grandpa has given us five pounds each for our birthday, and we thought it would be a lovely idea to spend it on presents for our guests.'

'We shall put them in the lucky dip and everyone will draw one out!' said Michael, doing a little dance of joy on the pavement. 'We're going to buy them now.'

'Dear me, what nice children to think of giving other people presents on their birthday,' thought Mr Pink-Whistle, who loved kind and generous people.

'Mother is making a big birthday cake with both our names on,' said Mollie. 'It's going to have pink icing. She saved up the sugar icing specially for us. And she is making pink, yellow, and red jellies, and two big chocolate puddings.'

'And we're going to play Blind-Man's Buff and Nuts-in-May, and Postman's Knock, and all kinds of games,' said Mike. 'And there are six boxes of crackers – what do you think of that? Won't everyone enjoy themselves?'

Mr Pink-Whistle walked along with the two happy children and watched them buy twelve lovely presents for their little friends. There was twenty pence over, and what do you think the children did with it?

'Let's buy twenty pence-worth of those pretty pink sweets and give them to this kind, little man,' whispered Mollie. 'I do like him!'

So, to Mr Pink-Whistle's great surprise he was given a bag of bright pink sweets by Mollie and Mike!

'Dear me!' he said. 'Dear me – how very sweet and kind of you! Just the sweets I like, too. Thank you very, very much indeed. I do hope you have a wonderful party on Thursday.'

Mr Pink-Whistle whispered magic words to himself when he went out of the shop, and disappeared. He wanted to follow the twins home and find out where they lived. He meant to give them a birthday present each.

So he trotted behind them, although they didn't know it, and saw the house they lived in. He wrote down the name of it in his notebook – *Fir-Tree House*.

When Thursday came, Mr Pink-Whistle bought two merry birthday cards, a big

farmyard for Michael with all kinds of little
animals in it, and a doll's house for Mollie,
full of the tiniest furniture. Then he set off to
Fir-Tree House, hoping that the children
would be in so that he could wish them many
happy returns of the day.

Their mother came to the door. Mr Pink-
Whistle raised his hat politely and asked to
see Mollie and Michael.

'Well – have you had whooping-cough?' asked Mrs Brown.

'Er – whooping-cough? What do you mean, exactly?' said Mr Pink-Whistle, very puzzled.

'You see, both the children have got whooping-cough now,' said Mrs Brown. 'The doctor came this morning and said they had caught it. It's such a pity, because it's their birthday, and they are so disappointed.'

'Can't they have their party then?' asked Mr Pink-Whistle.

'Oh no,' said Mrs Brown. 'They might give other children their cough. They mustn't have others here for a long time. And, you know, they had got such nice presents for their guests, and I have made a lovely cake and jellies and things, I am really as much disappointed and sad as Mollie and Mike are.'

'Are they in bed?' said Mr Pink-Whistle.

'No,' said Mrs Brown. 'They are not ill, but they just have a nasty cough. They are in the nursery. If you've had whooping-cough, you can go in and see them.'

'Oh, I've had whooping-cough all right,' said Mr Pink-Whistle. 'I had it when I was five. Yes – I'll go and see the children, please.'

So up into the big nursery he went – and, dear me, what sad children he found! Mollie wasn't smiling and Mike had quite lost his twinkle.

'Hello, hello!' said Pink-Whistle, bustling in. 'Many happy returns of the day! My, I'm sorry you've got whooping-cough!'

'It's so dreadfully horrid of it to have happened on our birthday!' said Mollie, trying not to cry. 'Why couldn't it have happened tomorrow? We've had our presents and our cards – but we can't have our friends here and let them share our cake and goodies and give them the lovely presents we bought. It doesn't seem fair, does it?'

'It doesn't, and it isn't,' said Mr Pink-Whistle sadly. 'Can't you really have any of your friends to tea?'

'No – because, you see, not one of them has had whooping-cough,' said Mike. 'But perhaps you would like to come, if you've had it?'

'Oh, I should. I certainly should,' said Mr Pink-Whistle, beaming. 'And do you know, I believe I could bring some guests who don't mind a scrap about whooping-cough – friends of my own, you know – very jolly ones.

Would you like that? Then you could have a party after all.'

'Ooooh – that would be fine,' said the twins, smiling in delight. 'Will you talk to Mother about it?'

So downstairs went Mr Pink-Whistle, leaving the two big parcels he had brought for Mollie and Mike to undo. He told the children's mother what he had said to the children, and she nodded her head.

'I am sure that the friends of a kind, little man like you would be nice to have,' she said.

'Bring twelve if you can, because I've got enough food for that number. I'll see you again at four o'clock, I hope.'

Off scurried Mr Pink-Whistle, back to his own little village. He burst in at his own tiny cottage, much to the surprise of Sooty, his big black cat.

'Sooty, Sooty!' cried Mr Pink-Whistle, 'We've got to find twelve people who have had whooping-cough or don't mind about it by four o'clock this afternoon. Will you help me?'

'Well, can't I be one?' asked Sooty at once. 'I don't mind about whooping-cough at all. Would they mind a cat coming?'

'No – I think they'd be pleased,' said Mr Pink-Whistle. 'I'll buy you a new blue party-bow. Now, come on – we must find some more people. What about little Mrs Tickle? She's sweet. And dear Mr Tiddly-Winks – I'm sure the twins would love him and his hat edged with tiddly-winks. Come on, Sooty!'

So off went the two to find more guests for the party. What a surprise for Mollie and Mike when they all arrived!

Now, when four o'clock came, you should have seen the twelve people that went trooping up the garden path of the children's house.

First there was Mr Pink-Whistle himself, of course, beaming all over his plump face, his green eyes shining. Behind him came Sooty, the cat, with a new blue party-bow tied very beautifully.

Then came Mrs Tickle, a darling little person with such tiny feet that when she walked it seemed almost as if she was running by clockwork. There was Mr Tiddly-Winks, a tall thin man whose hat was sewn with red, green, blue, and yellow tiddly-wink counters that jiggled and clattered as he walked.

That was four. The fifth person was the pixie, Tiptoe, who had tucked her wings inside her cloak so that no one in the street should see them. The sixth and seventh guests were two big sandy rabbits, looking rather shy but very pleased, each with a pink bow round his neck.

The eighth guest was a brownie whose beard was so long that he tied it round his waist when he walked, in case he tripped over it. The ninth and tenth were Mr and Mrs Roundy, who were just like their name; and the eleventh and twelfth were two goblin children, all dressed up in their best. They were not very pretty, for their noses turned up and they had such big ears – but they were so smiley that no one could help liking them.

Mrs Brown was most astonished to see such a strange company – especially the cat and the rabbits – but she was too polite to say anything, and helped the goblin children off with their coats.

Well! When Mollie and Michael saw their strange guests trooping into the nursery, they were most excited and pleased. Gracious! What a marvellous party it would be, with rabbits and a cat, and goblin children and a pixie, and the rest.

Everyone had a present to give to Mollie and Michael, of course, though the rabbits only brought a bunch of early primroses each, which they thought were not very good presents – but the twins simply loved the pretty, pale yellow flowers, and Mollie put them into a little blue bowl at once, in the very middle of the birthday table.

You should have seen some of the presents that the guests gave to the children. Mr and Mrs Roundy gave them a dear little mug each, and as soon as it was lifted up to drink from, each mug played a tune. Mollie's played 'Sing a Song of Sixpence', and Mike's played 'Humpty-Dumpty'.

'I shall drink all day long now,' said Mike. 'I think my mug must be magic.'

Mr Tiddly-Winks gave them a set of beautiful tiddly-winks each, of course, and Sooty, the cat, gave them a black china cat exactly like herself – and it mewed when its tail was pulled. So you can guess that it mewed all the afternoon, because somebody or other was always pulling its tail. It really was great fun.

Well, Mrs Brown and the twins soon got used to such strange guests, and the party began. Goodness, it was fun to play Nuts-in-May with the rabbits and the cat, and Blind-Man's Buff with Mr Pink-Whistle as the blind man. He kept catching Mrs Roundy, who was a dreadful giggler and could never get out of the way in time.

The tea was gorgeous, because Mrs Tickle had brought along a big tin of her best home-made biscuits, and as they were all made in the shape of toys, with jam right in the middle, they were most exciting.

Mike had a biscuit just like a train, and

when he squeezed it, the jam came out of the funnel. Everyone thought it was wonderful.

Then they had the lucky dip – and how all the guests loved their presents! Sooty got a clockwork mouse, and when Mike wound it up and set it going Sooty was quite mad with delight, and chased the mouse under chairs and tables till Mrs Brown felt quite giddy to watch her.

'I think this is the finest party anyone ever had,' said Mollie happily. 'Fancy finding twelve guests who don't mind about whooping-cough! I am sorry we couldn't have our proper friends – but I can't help thinking this is a more exciting party with this sort of guests, Mike.'

Mr Pink-Whistle was asked to do a little magic, because the twins knew now that he was half-magic.

So he was most obliging, and kept appearing and disappearing in a most surprising way. Mollie begged him to whisper the magic words in her ear, so that she could make herself disappear too – but she didn't get them quite right, and to everyone's great astonishment only her legs disappeared.

And there was Mollie running about the room without any legs that could be seen. Mrs Roundy laughed till she cried.

Then they had the crackers. Sooty and the rabbits had never seen crackers before, and when the first one went off BANG, they were dreadfully frightened. Sooty jumped up the chimney at once, and the two rabbits rushed under the sofa.

When Sooty came down at last, she was just as sooty as her name, and Mrs Brown had to hold her under the tap and scrub her clean. Then she sat in front of the fire to be dried, whilst the two rabbits crept out from the sofa and wondered if they dared to pull a cracker themselves.

'Well, let's,' said the bigger rabbit. 'There are caps inside, Whiskers, dear – and you know I've always wanted some sort of hat to wear.'

So they pulled a cracker, and then another, and out came a blue bonnet for Whiskers and a golden crown for Floppy. Goodness, they were pleased.

Then they played tiddly-winks – and you should have seen the way Mr Tiddly-Winks played. He was simply marvellous. He could not only flip counters into the cup – he could flip just anything.

'Flip this pencil,' said Mike, and Mr Tiddly-Winks flipped it – and it hopped straight into the cup. Then he flipped the poker, and that went into the cup and stood itself quite upright. Then he flipped one of the little dolls out of the doll's house, and she flipped into the cup and sat there, looking very comfortable.

'You *are* clever,' said Mike. 'I wish I could play tiddly-winks like that.'

Then Mr Pink-Whistle looked at his watch. 'Dear me!' he said. 'We must all go. We have to catch the bus. Goodbye, Mollie dear; goodbye, Mike. We've had a wonderful party, and we thank you very much for such a good time.'

'Thank you for bringing such a lovely lot of guests,' said the twins, and they kissed everyone goodbye – even Sooty, who was terribly proud of being hugged by the two children.

Then they all trooped off to catch a most peculiar yellow-and-purple bus that stopped outside. Mike and Mollie had never seen it before, so they thought it must be a special bus sent to fetch their strange guests. They waved goodbye to them and then looked at one another.

'Dear old Pink-Whistle,' said Mollie. 'Isn't he a darling! He's just the kindest fellow in all the world. When things seemed too horrid for words, he came along and put everything right. I wish I was like him.'

'Goodbye, goodbye!' shouted Mike, waving to Mr Pink-Whistle, who was the last one to get into the bus. 'Take care of yourself, Mr Pink-Whistle, and *do* come and see us again!'

Goodbye! Goodbye!

Chapter 3

A Puzzle for the Jones Family

One afternoon, when Mr Pink-Whistle was walking down a town street, trying to find a tea-shop where he could have a bun and a cup of coffee, he heard a mew coming from the small front garden of a house.

Mr Pink-Whistle stopped at once. He knew that the mew was from a cat in need of help. Surely it couldn't have been caught in a trap? He opened the gate of the garden and went inside.

A tabby-cat was sitting on the front doorstep of the house mewing pitifully. She was thin and looked very lonely and miserable.

'Poor creature! Won't your family let you in?' said Mr Pink-Whistle. 'I'll ring the bell and tell them. And I'll tell them to give you a good meal, too. You look so thin!'

Mr Pink-Whistle rang the bell loudly. Nobody came to the door. He knocked with the knocker, blim, blam, blim, blam! Nobody came. Then Pink-Whistle saw that the blinds were drawn down, and that the knocker wasn't cleaned, and that an old newspaper lay on the front-door mat.

'Why, they must be away!' he thought. And just as he thought that, a voice came from over the fence next door.

'Hi! It's no use knocking! The Jones family are away! They've been away two weeks and are coming back tomorrow.'

'Thank you,' said Pink-Whistle, nodding to the boy who looked over the fence. Then he spoke to the cat. 'And what have you been doing to get yourself so thin and miserable in two weeks, Tabby?'

'Well, my family went without leaving anywhere for me to sleep, and without arranging for any food for me,' said Tabby mournfully. 'I've had hardly anything for my dinner for two weeks, and though I've tried to catch a few mice, it is difficult, because there are hardly any round here. So I've got thin. But what has made me so miserable is that the family I love should treat me like this! It isn't fair.'

'Indeed it isn't!' said Pink-Whistle in a rage. 'What! This horrid family went away and left you all alone and uncared for! I won't have it! I'll go straight to the fish shop and buy you some fish!'

So off went the angry, little man, with the

tabby-cat running at his heels, tail well up in the air. Pink-Whistle bought a fine bit of fish and took it back to the cat's garden. The tabby gobbled up the fish, uncooked as it was, and then began to wash itself, looking pleased and happy.

'Now look here, Tabby – I'm going to show that horrid family called Jones what it's like to have no food!' said Mr Pink-Whistle fiercely. 'You just wait till they come home tomorrow. I'll show them! I'll show them!'

The next day was Saturday. The family were coming home after tea, and they had written to ask the milkman to send some milk, the baker to send some bread, the greengrocer to leave some potatoes, the butcher to leave some meat, and the grocer to leave butter, tea and the rest of the things.

There was a little yard at the back, with a big box in which the tradespeople left their goods if there was no one to take them in at the back door. Each man left his goods in the box and shut down the lid. Mr Pink-Whistle soon found out where the box was, because he made himself invisible and watched where the goods were put.

And then the sly, little man opened the lid

of the box, took out everything, popped them into an enormous bag he had brought, and ran off down the street. The tabby-cat watched him in amazement.

Pink-Whistle went to a row of poor, old tumbledown cottages. In them lived three or four poor families whose children went barefoot. Pink-Whistle had a fine time there. Do you know what he did?

He opened each door of the row of cottages and popped inside the kitchen something that he had taken out of the box in the back yard! Mrs Tibbles got two loaves of bread. Goodness, wasn't she surprised to see the door open and the loaves hop into the kitchen! She couldn't see Pink-Whistle, of course, because he was quite invisible.

Mrs Harris, next door, was peeling potatoes at the sink when she saw her door open and a bottle of milk and a large piece of meat come in. She squealed and dropped the potato knife. But she soon got over her fright when she found that the milk and meat stayed on the floor, waiting to be picked up!

Everyone in the row got something. Then Pink-Whistle hurried off to the house again. The Jones family had just come back and were busy unpacking upstairs. The cat was mewing and purring round them, delighted to see the family again, although they had treated her so badly.

It was half-past six. Mrs Jones went out into the yard to fetch in the food, meaning to get Mr Jones, Joan Jones, and John Jones some supper. But there was nothing at all in the box. How angry she was!

She flew upstairs and said that Mr Jones couldn't possibly have posted her cards to the tradesmen, asking them to send the goods. They quarrelled, and then at last John Jones was sent out to see what food he could get before the shops closed.

The dairy was shut, so he could get no milk. The baker had only one stale brown loaf left, and John bought that. He bought a string of sausages, some butter, some bacon and some eggs. Then back he went home.

'Put them in the larder,' called Mrs Jones. 'I'm just coming. Don't leave them on the table or the cat will get them, the greedy thing!'

The cat didn't get them – but someone else did!

Mr Pink-Whistle, quite unseen, slipped into

the kitchen and went to the larder. In a second everything was under his arm, in his big bag! The little man slipped out again – and back to those poor cottages he went, chuckling away to himself.

And what a pleasant surprise the cottagers got again, when eggs, sausages, bread, bacon and butter suddenly appeared round their doors! They couldn't make it out. They ran to the door to see who had put the things there, but they could see no one. Mr Pink-Whistle was invisible. All they heard was a deep chuckle from somewhere near by. It was very puzzling – but very nice!

Well, the Jones family were in a state when they found that the larder was empty. Not a thing was there!

'Did you put the things in the larder as I told you?' asked Mrs Jones. John nodded.

'Of course I did,' he said. 'And shut the door, too. So the cat couldn't have got them.'

'Well, the shops will all be shut now,' said his mother. 'We can't get any food for supper. Your father will have to run round to the dairy early tomorrow morning and get some eggs, milk and butter. We can at least make some sort of breakfast then. And maybe the butcher has some meat over that he can let us have.'

Well, Mr Jones did manage to get some eggs, milk, butter and a loaf of bread from a neighbour in the morning. He put the loaf on the table, Mrs Jones popped the eggs into a saucepan to boil, put the butter into a dish, and the milk into a jug.

But as soon as she turned her back, the things were gone! Yes – the eggs were whisked out of the saucepan, the loaf disappeared with the butter and milk, and when the Jones

174

family came to breakfast, there wasn't anything for them to have at all! Mr Pink-Whistle had been along again! Only the tabby knew what was happening, for, like all animals, she had a strong sense of smell and could smell him even though he was invisible.

There was such a wailing and crying when the children found there was no breakfast. 'We had no supper yesterday – and now no breakfast today!' they wept. 'What is happening? This is simply horrid.'

The butcher let them have some meat although it was Sunday. Mr Jones got a cabbage from the garden, and Mrs Jones borrowed some flour from a neighbour to make a batter pudding. Everything was put on to cook. The joint sizzled in the oven, and the cabbage boiled in its saucepan. The pudding browned nicely by the meat.

'Goodness! I've never been so hungry in all my life!' said Joan. 'I do hope dinner will be early!'

But gracious me, when Mrs Jones went into the garden for a moment, Pink-Whistle slipped indoors, whipped the meat out of the oven, took the cabbage out of the saucepan, and popped the pudding into a dish he carried. Then off he went again to the row of tumble-down cottages. The people there really thought that they must have gone mad when a large, half-cooked joint appeared, a tender cabbage, and a big batter pudding!

But oh, the Jones family! What a state they were in! How they sobbed and cried, all except Mr Jones who wondered what in the world could be happening. The tabby-cat sat and watched them.

'I'm so hungry,' wept Joan. The tabby suddenly got up and went outside. She saw

Pink-Whistle sitting on the wall and went up to him.

'Please, Mr Pink-Whistle,' she said, 'don't punish my family any more. I can't bear it. They are all so hungry, and I know what it is to be hungry. I thought I would be pleased when I saw them getting as thin and miserable as I got when they were away. But I find that I am not pleased. I am only sorry.'

'You are a good and kind, little cat,' said Pink-Whistle, jumping down from the wall. 'I think you are right. We won't punish them any more. I will get them some food and speak a few words to them.'

Pink-Whistle went to a tea shop that was open and bought eight buns. He took them into the house and put the bag on the table. Everyone was most surprised to see the bag appear out of the air, because they couldn't see Pink-Whistle, of course.

'Look – what is it – how did it come – oh, who put that bag there?' cried the Jones family.

'I did!' said Pink-Whistle, making his voice very deep and solemn. 'I'm Pink-Whistle, your cat's good friend. You left her without food for two weeks – so I took away *your* food

177

to make you feel what it was like to be hungry and not to have anything to eat. But your cat is sorry for you, and so I will not punish you any more. I have brought you something to eat. Look after your cat in future, or you will be *very sorry*!'

There was a silence after this speech. It seemed to come out of the air, and was very strange to the Jones family. They stood or sat, their eyes wide open, wondering who was speaking. Then they opened the bag. There were only eight buns there – but, dear me, how pleased everyone was to see them!

And you will be glad to know that each of the Jones family felt ashamed of having left their poor cat without food or sleeping-place, and they gave her a bit of their buns. She is happy now, and always on the look-out for her good friend, Mr Pink-Whistle. When she sees him coming she runs up to his legs, rubs against them, and purrs. And if he is invisible, it *does* look funny to *see* Tabby rubbing herself against nothing! You would laugh if you saw her!

Chapter 4

Mr Pink-Whistle's Circus

There was once a little girl called Eileen, who was feeling very excited because she had been asked to go to the circus.

Her friend was going with her mother, and they asked Eileen to go, too. So she was very happy, and she counted the days till the Great Day came.

'Mother, it's Galliano's Circus,' she said happily. 'I shall see Lotta on her horse, Black Beauty, and I shall see Jimmy and his performing dog, Lucky. I shall see Jumbo, the dear old elephant, playing cricket with his keeper, and I shall see Lilliput and all his monkeys. Oh, won't it be fun?'

The day came at last. Eileen woke up – but oh, what a pity, she had a horrid sore feeling

179

in her throat that made her choke and cough. Mother heard her and came in.

'Have you got a sore throat?' she asked Eileen. The little girl didn't want to say yes, because she knew that sore throats meant being kept in bed – but she always told her mother the truth, so she nodded her head.

'It's not very bad, Mother,' she said. 'It won't stop me going to the circus. I can hardly feel it.'

Then she coughed again, and that hurt her throat. Mother made her open her mouth.

'Oh, darling,' she said, 'you really have got a very nasty throat. I simply daren't let you go today. And, besides, Mary might catch it if you go with her. You can't possibly go out – you must stay in bed.'

Poor Eileen. She began to cry bitterly, and buried her face in her pillow. 'It's not fair,' she wept. 'Just the very day I was going to the circus – the *very* day! Oh, I do feel so unhappy. Now Mary will go without me. They will take someone else. Somebody else will have my treat. Mother, It's *not fair.*'

'No – it doesn't seem fair, darling,' said Mother. 'But things aren't always fair, you know. Cheer up. I will go out and buy you a toy this afternoon when you sleep. Then you shall have it at tea-time.'

Mother went out of the room. Eileen cried for a little while, then she fell asleep. She didn't want any breakfast, and she didn't want any dinner. Her throat hurt her. She was cross and miserable. When Mother tucked her up for an afternoon rest, Eileen began to sob again.

'Mary and her mother are just starting out for the circus. They're catching the bus. Mother, it isn't fair!'

'Now don't cry any more or you won't sleep,' said Mother, and she went to the door. 'I'm just going out to buy you a surprise.'

Eileen heard the front door bang. She tried to go to sleep, but she couldn't. She kept thinking of Mary. Now they would have arrived at the circus. Now they would be taking their seats round the ring. Now the band would play.

She began to cry again. She wasn't really a cry-baby, but when you feel ill you can't help crying at all kinds of things, can you?

'I don't think it's a bit fair,' wept the little girl. 'I don't, I don't.'

Now who should come along under the window at that very minute but dear old Mr Pink-Whistle! You know how he loves to put things right, if he can – so you can guess that he stopped at once and listened.

'A little girl in trouble!' he said to himself. 'I must look into this!'

He went to the front door and pushed it. It opened to him, for he was half-magic. Up the stairs he went and into Eileen's room. The little girl heard him opening the door, and she stared at him in surprise, for he had the green eyes and pointed ears of the fairy-folk.

'Hello,' said Mr Pink-Whistle. 'What's the trouble?'

'I was going to the circus today – but now I've got a bad throat and I can't,' said Eileen, the tears running down her cheeks again. 'Who are you? I like you.'

'I'm Mr Pink-Whistle,' said the little man. 'I like you, too. I think you would be quite pretty if you didn't spoil your face with crying.'

'Well, you'd cry, too, if you couldn't go to the circus after all,' said Eileen. 'I just simply can't help it. I keep thinking of it.'

'I suppose you wouldn't like to see my circus, would you?' suddenly asked Mr Pink-Whistle. 'I mean I'm sure it isn't as good as Galliano's – but it's quite fun.'

'But how can I see it if I'm in bed?' said Eileen in astonishment.

'Easily!' said Pink-Whistle. 'There's room on your bed for my circus to perform. Do you mind putting your legs down flat? That's right. Now look – this is the ring – and you are the people looking on, so you must clap when anything good is done.'

'But where's the circus?' asked Eileen.

'Just a minute, just a minute,' said Mr Pink-

Whistle, and he ran into the room next door, which was Eileen's playroom. There were plenty of toys there and it didn't take Pink-Whistle long to rub a little magic on to the ones he wanted for his circus! His magic made them all come alive, and in half a minute he had told them all what to do. Then he went back into the bedroom.

'The circus is coming!' he said. 'Listen to the band!'

In came the band! It was the baby doll carrying the musical box, playing a merry tune by turning the handle round and round – and the pink cat playing the little drum in time to the tune – rum-ti-tum-ti-tum, tum-ti-tum-ti-tum! They climbed up on to the bed and settled down to play their little band together. Eileen was so surprised!

Then in came the toy elephant, Jumbo, led by his keeper, one of the boy-dolls! They climbed up on to the bed, too, and to Eileen's great joy they played cricket together just like the real Jumbo and his keeper at the big circus. Her toy elephant was very clever at hitting the ball that the doll threw to him, and once he hit it so hard that it bounced on Mr Pink-Whistle's nose with a loud 'ping'!

That made everyone laugh. Eileen clapped loudly. 'Now come the next performers,' said Pink-Whistle. The band struck up a merry tune again, and rum-ti-tum-ti-tum went the drum. In came the sailor doll with all the teddy bears tied together in a row.

'The performing bears!' said Pink-Whistle. 'Play up, band – the bears want to dance!'

Well, those teddy bears did dance! They danced all over the bed, they rolled about, they grunted and growled, and they had just as good a time as Eileen herself had.

'Well, I'd no idea my bears could be so funny, Mr Pink-Whistle!' she said. 'If I laugh much more I'll get a stitch in my side.'

Then in galloped the little, brown horse without the wooden cart it usually pulled along. Riding on its back was the fairy doll! She did look simply lovely, and Eileen was most surprised to see how clever she was! She stood up on the horse's back, and galloped over the bed like that. Then she stood on one leg only and didn't fall off once.

'Marvellous!' said Eileen. 'Oh, Mr Pink-Whistle, this is simply lovely. What's next?'

'Your two monkeys come next,' said the little man. 'Here they are.'

And in they came, grinning all over their faces. What a time they had! They didn't stay on the bed. They leapt all over the room, and swung by their tails from the lamp that hung down from the ceiling. They climbed all over Pink-Whistle, and when he took some bananas from his pocket and gave them to the monkeys, they peeled them neatly and gobbled them up.

'Aren't they clever?' said Eileen. 'Oh, Mr Pink-Whistle, I think I'd rather see your circus than even Mr Galliano's – because, you see, your circus is made of all my own toys, and I really didn't know they were so clever. Oh, look – here come all my toy soldiers on horseback!'

The soldiers galloped in. The band struck up again – and hey presto, all those horses began to dance prettily round the bed in time to the music – just like the horses do in any circus. It was marvellous to watch. Suddenly the front door opened. It was Mother back from her walk. Eileen stared at Mr Pink-Whistle.

'That's Mother!' she said. 'I wonder what she's brought me. Oh, Mr Pink-Whistle, do stay and let her see the circus, too.'

'Sorry, little girl, I can't,' said Pink-Whistle. 'I don't want your mother to see me. I'm going to disappear and slip down the stairs. Watch me!'

Eileen watched him – and to her amazement the merry little man seemed to dissolve like sugar in a cup – and then he wasn't there at all! But his voice came to her from near the door.

'Goodbye. So glad you liked my circus. Do things seem a bit fairer now?'

'Oh, yes!' cried Eileen. And then down the stairs went Pink-Whistle, opened the front door, and was gone. Mother saw the front door opening and shutting by itself and she was most surprised. You see, she couldn't see Pink-Whistle at all.

She went up the stairs – and as soon as she came to Eileen's door, an extraordinary thing happened. All the toys had hopped down from Eileen's bed and were running back to the nursery. There they went – monkeys, dolls, bears and all. Mother simply couldn't believe her eyes.

'I must be imagining things,' she thought. She peeped into the nursery. All the toys were in their places, as still as could be. Nobody could ever imagine they had been in Mr Pink-Whistle's circus all afternoon. 'Eileen! What do you think I've bought you?' cried Mother, going into the bedroom. 'Look – a little toy circus! Won't you love that?'

'Yes, I will,' said Eileen, sitting up joyfully. 'But Mother – I shall always like Mr Pink-Whistle's circus the very best of all!'

And I'm sure I would, too, wouldn't you?

Chapter 5

Mr Pink-Whistle and the Cowards

Paul went to school every morning, feeling afraid. He wasn't afraid of school, or of his teacher, or of any of his lessons. He was afraid of two boys who went to the same school as he did.

Every morning these two boys lay in wait for Paul. He had to go down their lane, and sometimes they hid behind the big oak tree to jump out at him, and sometimes they hid behind the hedge. He never knew where they would be.

They never hurt him. They didn't kick or pinch or punch – they teased Paul in another way.

They threw his school cap over the hedge or up into a tree. They threw his school bag into the pond. They would take his lunch and scatter it over the grass. And Paul couldn't possibly stop them.

'You are cowards,' he once said to John and Alan. 'You wouldn't do this to me if there was only one of you, because I could fight you then. But I can't fight two of you. I shall report you to our teacher if you do this any more.'

'Well, if you tell tales, we'll tease you all the more,' said Alan.

'We might even take off your shoes and socks and put them on the old goat over there,' said John.

Well, Paul knew quite well that they were likely to do what they said, for they didn't seem to care a bit what they did. So he didn't tell. He didn't like telling tales anyway, but he became very miserable about his teasing, because he got into trouble at home and at school over his lost caps, his wet school bag and books, and his excuses over his lost lunch.

'Surely there must be times when it's best to tell tales?' he thought to himself. 'Why should I keep getting into trouble like this for things that are not my fault? Still – I should get into worse trouble from John and Alan if they knew I'd told tales – they might begin to pinch and kick me. I'm too small to fight both of them at once.'

Well, things went on like this all through the summer term. Poor Paul had to have two new caps, because John threw one of his into the middle of a gorse bush far too prickly to rescue it from, and then Alan threw the second cap up a telegraph post and it hung there on the top of the post, impossible to reach.

Twice Paul was scolded and punished for bringing school books soaking wet to school. But how could he help it? John had again thrown his bag into the pond, scaring all the ducks, and soaking everything inside the bag.

And then one day something happened. Paul was going along to school, a little earlier than usual, hoping to slip down the lane before John and Alan came along. And up the lane came a funny, little man, whose pointed ears showed that he was half a brownie.

It was Mr Pink-Whistle, of course, but

nobody could know it was because he
couldn't be seen. He was invisible, but he had
quite forgotten that, and was stamping along
gaily, whistling loudly.

Now, half-way down the lane John and Alan
were hiding behind a tree, waiting for Paul,
and when they heard the footsteps and the
whistling they felt sure it was Paul coming
along as usual. So, to Mr Pink-Whistle's
enormous astonishment, the two boys
suddenly leapt out as he came by, shouting
fiercely, their arms outstretched to catch

Paul. But Paul wasn't there – no one was there! They couldn't see Pink-Whistle – and they couldn't hear him either, now, for he had stopped walking in amazement and was no longer whistling.

'Well,' said John, in astonishment, 'I thought I heard Paul. But there's no one here!'

'I heard steps and whistling,' said Alan. 'Oh, look – there's Paul – coming down the lane. Come on, let's give his mac to the old goat to eat! Before Paul can get it away from him, he'll have munched big holes in it!'

Mr Pink-Whistle listened to all this in the greatest surprise. Give a mackintosh to a goat to eat? These boys must be mad!

John and Alan pounced on poor Paul. They dragged his dark blue mac off his arm. 'The old goat wants it for his dinner!' said Alan, with a grin.

'No don't,' said Paul, in alarm. 'My mother has just paid a lot of money for that mac. It's new. Don't be so mean.'

But the mac was wrenched away and thrown over the hedge for the goat to eat. Paul was left to try and get it back whilst the other boys ran off to school, laughing.

'Beasts!' said Paul, climbing over the hedge to get his mac. The goat had already bitten off a button. 'Why don't they leave me alone? They throw my caps away, they throw my bag into the pond, they spoil everything of mine that they can. And I can't stop them! Nobody can!'

'Excuse me – but I think I can do something about it,' said Mr Pink-Whistle, appearing so suddenly that both Paul and the goat jumped in surprise. The goat dropped the mac and ran away. Paul stood and stared at Pink-Whistle in amazement.

'Where did you come from?' he asked. 'You suddenly appeared!'

'Yes. I forgot I was invisible,' said Pink-Whistle. 'I didn't mean to give you quite such a shock. Let me have a look at that mac.'

There was a big tear in it and a button was gone. It was in the goat, so there was no getting that back. But somehow Pink-Whistle managed to mend the mac. A new button seemed to grow in the right place, and the big tear pressed its edges together, gave a peculiar kind of squeak and disappeared.

'I say,' said Paul, half-scared. 'I say – you're a bit magic, aren't you?'

'Just a bit,' said Pink-Whistle. 'Now – you'd better rush off to school, or you'll be late. Leave things to me. I have a feeling I'm going to interfere a little. If you want to see a bit of fun, hide behind that tree at the end of the morning.'

Paul stared hard at Pink-Whistle. He couldn't make him out. He liked the little man very much indeed, and he thought he had the brightest twinkle in his eyes that he had ever seen. He nodded, put his mac over his arm, and sped off to school, wondering what was going to happen.

At the end of the morning Paul shot off before John and Alan left. Now it was his turn to hide behind the tree – not to pounce out, but to watch. He couldn't see Mr Pink-Whistle anywhere. He wondered if he could have imagined him.

But Pink-Whistle was there all right. He had made himself invisible again, that was all. He waited for John and Alan, and very soon along they came, kicking a stone between them.

'Excuse me,' said Pink-Whistle, in a loud but polite voice. The boys stopped in surprise. They could see no one.

'I want to borrow your caps,' said Pink-Whistle, still very polite. To the two boys' dismay their caps suddenly whisked off their heads, flew up into the air and landed on the exact tops of two chimneys belonging to a nearby cottage.

'And now your shoes, please,' said Pink-Whistle, and their laces were undone, and their shoes pulled off, before they knew what was happening!

Up into the air went the four shoes. Two landed on the old billy-goat's horns and two on the horns of a most astonished cow.

Neither of the boys dared go and get them. The cow looked angry and the goat knew how to butt very hard.

'Fine,' said Pink-Whistle, who still couldn't be seen. 'So kind of you to let me have your things. But still, why not? You take Paul's things, don't you? So, of course, you are willing to lend me yours.'

'Who's speaking? Who's doing all this?' said John, clutching Alan's arm.

Behind the tree there sounded a chuckle. It came from Paul, who was really enjoying himself. Now Alan and John knew what it was like to be teased and not be able to stop the teaser!

Mr Pink-Whistle hadn't nearly finished. No, when he did a thing he did it really thoroughly!

He stripped off the boys' socks next, made the billy-goat stand still, and then slipped them on to each leg. The goat was rather pleased. The socks were warm, he felt grand in them, and he could always eat them when he was tired of them. He trotted round the field in them looking rather peculiar because he still had a pair of shoes on his horns.

Alan and John were very scared by now,

and began to run away. But a strong and firm hand took hold of each of them.

'No, don't go. I would like to borrow your school bags, please.'

So off came their school satchels. One sailed away to the top of a tall chestnut tree, and the other fell into the stream and sailed down it merrily, with pens, pencils and papers leaking out of it. Oh dear, now they couldn't do their homework, and the teacher would be very angry!

Their ties came off next, flew up towards the telegraph wires and then tied themselves round a wire in neat bows. It was really most extraordinary. Even Paul forgot to laugh for a moment and felt a bit scared. This little invisible man must know a lot of magic!

'Don't!' begged Alan, in alarm, holding on to his coat and shorts, afraid that they would go next. 'Don't! Who are you, doing this? Don't do any more!'

Mr Pink-Whistle hadn't quite finished. He pulled out the boys' handkerchiefs, threw them into the field, and the goat at once ate them both. He didn't really mind what he ate. He had once tried to eat a tin and many times he had eaten newspapers, rope, paper-bags, and cardboard cartons. So he was quite pleased with the handkerchiefs.

'Well, thank you very much,' said Mr Pink-Whistle politely. 'That's all for this morning. I'll meet you here again another day perhaps. That would be very nice.'

'No, oh no!' cried Alan and John, and fled down the lane in their bare feet as fast as they could go. Paul came out from behind the tree, laughing.

'I don't know quite where you are,' he said to Mr Pink-Whistle, who was still invisible, 'but thank you very much for interfering. Oh dear, look at those caps on the chimneys still.'

Pink-Whistle suddenly appeared, looking very pleased with himself. 'Yes, they look comic up there, don't they?' he said. 'I did enjoy myself. Well, my boy, I have a feeling that those two boys won't tease you much more. I don't believe they liked my bit of interference! I'll be along here again for the next few days, so call out if you want me.'

But Paul didn't call out, because John and Alan never went down that lane again. They were so afraid of meeting the polite and powerful, little, invisible man that they went another way to school. It took them twice as long, so they had to start much earlier. Paul never had any bother with them again.

The funny thing is the school ties are still tied in bows round the telegraph wire. Nobody can imagine who put them there – but if you see them you'll know. It was all because Mr Pink-Whistle interfered!

Chapter 6

Mr Pink-Whistle
and the Money-Box

For some time Mr Pink-Whistle hadn't come across anything to put right, and he was feeling very pleased about it.

'Perhaps the world is getting a better place,' he thought to himself. 'Perhaps people are being nicer to one another, and kinder. Maybe I needn't go around any more looking for things to put right. Perhaps I can go back to my own little cottage and live there peacefully with Sooty, my cat.'

But that very day Pink-Whistle had to change his mind, because he found two very unhappy children.

Pink-Whistle was walking in the lane that

ran at the back of their garden, and he heard one of the children crying.

'Never mind,' said a boy's voice. 'Never mind, Katie. We shall have to save up again, that's all.'

'But it was such a mean thing to do to us,' sobbed Katie. 'That's what's making me cry. It was such a horrid, mean, unkind thing.'

Pink-Whistle peeped over the wall. He saw two children nearby – a boy and a girl. They both looked very upset, but the boy wasn't crying.

'What's the matter?' asked Pink-Whistle. 'Can I do anything to help?'

'No, I'm afraid not,' said the boy. 'You see, it's like this. Katie and I have been saving up for our mother's birthday – we know exactly what she wants – that big red shawl in the draper's. It's a lovely one.'

'I know. I've seen it,' said Pink-Whistle.

'Well, it costs a lot of money,' said the boy. 'But Katie and I have been doing all kinds of jobs to earn the money for it.'

'We ran errands and we delivered papers,' said Katie, rubbing her eyes.

'I helped the farmer to lift his potatoes,' said the boy. 'And that's hard work.'

'And I took Mrs Brown's baby out each day for a week when she was ill,' said Katie. 'She gave me fifty pence for that.'

'And I weeded old Mr Kent's garden, and he gave me a pound,' said the boy. 'We put it all into our money-box pig.'

'Oh, was your money-box in the shape of a pig?' asked Mr Pink-Whistle. 'I like that sort of money-box.'

'It was a tin pig, painted pink, and it had a slit in its back,' said Katie. 'And it had a little key hanging on its tail to unlock a sort of little door in its tummy. We got the money out of the little door when we wanted it.'

'The pig was so nice and full,' said the boy. 'It jingled when we shook it. We were sure we had nearly enough to buy the shawl, and it is Mother's birthday next week. But now all our money is gone!'

'Where's it gone?' said Pink-Whistle, surprised.

'Someone stole it,' said Katie, her eyes filling with tears again. 'We took it out here in the garden, meaning to count out the money. Then Mother called us in for our biscuits and we ran indoors, and when we came out the pig was gone, and all the money with it.'

'Somebody must have come by, looked over the wall, and seen the money-box pig,' said the boy, sadly. 'Now all our hard work is wasted – and we shall never get enough money to buy that shawl.'

'It really is a shame,' said Mr Pink-Whistle, getting quite red with anger. 'It's not fair that someone should come along and take all the money you've worked hard to get. Perhaps I have got some for you. Wait a minute. Let me look in my pockets.'

But Pink-Whistle had only ten pence that day, so that wasn't much use. He rubbed one of his pointed ears and frowned. What could he do? He must do something!

Someone called the children. 'We must go,' said Katie. 'It's time for our dinner. Thank you for being so nice.'

The children ran off. Mr Pink-Whistle went on down the lane, remembering the girl's tear-stained face and the boy's look of disappointment. What a shame to steal from children!

'Well, I shall do something!' said Pink-Whistle, fiercely. 'But I don't know what. It seems to me as if all I can do is to poke my nose into every house I see, and try to find that money-box pig!'

So he made himself invisible, and began to peep into the windows of all the houses he passed. But he didn't see any money-box pig at all.

He went on and on, peering into kitchens and sitting-rooms, trying to discover a money-box pig – and at last he found one!

It was standing on the mantelpiece of a neat little cottage, next to a ticking clock. There was a man in the room, reading. He looked smart and clean and neat – but Pink-Whistle didn't really like his face.

'Too clever!' thought Pink-Whistle. 'Too sharp! He looks as if he would do people a bad turn if he could, and think himself clever to do it! And there's the money-box pig, standing on the mantelpiece. Can it be the pig the children had stolen from them? Surely this well-dressed man here wouldn't steal such a thing as a child's money-box. He looks quite well-off.'

Someone went up the path and knocked at the door. The man inside looked up, got up quickly, took the money-box pig and put it under a cushion. Then Pink-Whistle knew he had stolen it. 'Aha!' said the little man to himself, 'Aha! He wouldn't hide it if he hadn't stolen it. The mean fellow!'

The man opened the door to his friend, and Pink-Whistle slipped in beside him. He was quite invisible, so no one knew he was there.

'You're early,' said the first man, 'The others haven't arrived yet.'

'Oho!' thought Pink-Whistle, 'so there is to be a meeting. I think I'll stay – and have a bit of fun!'

So he stood in a corner, and then, when he had a chance to do it, he slipped his hand under the cushion and took out the pig. He stood it on the mantelpiece.

He shook it and the money jingled. Then Pink-Whistle made a grunting noise, just like a little pig, and spoke in a funny, piggy voice.

'Take me back, take me back!'

Mr Crooky, the man who lived in the cottage, looked up, very startled, and so did his friend. It seemed to them as if the money-box pig on the mantelpiece was jigging up and down and talking. They couldn't see Pink-Whistle moving it, of course.

'How extraordinary!' said the friend. Mr Crooky got up and took hold of the pig very roughly. He took it into the kitchen and put it on the dresser there. He slammed the door and came back. There was a knock at the front door and two more men came into the meeting.

Pink-Whistle grinned. He slipped quietly into the kitchen found the pig, came back, shut the kitchen door softly, and, when no one was looking, placed the pig on the mantelpiece again!

Then he jiggled it hard and grunted in a

piggy way again, talking in a funny, squeaky voice. 'Take me back! Take me back! I don't belong to you. Take me back!'

All the four men stopped talking and stared in astonishment at the jigging pig. Mr Crooky went very red and looked most alarmed. How had that pig got down from the dresser, opened the kitchen door, and got back to the mantelpiece? How was it that it grunted and jigged and talked like that? It must be magic!

'What does it mean, saying that it wants to

be taken back?' asked one of the men. 'Doesn't it belong to you?'

'Of course it does,' said Mr Crooky. 'I can't imagine what's come over the pig. I never knew a tin pig behave like that before.'

'Oh, you bad story-teller, oh, you wicked man!' squeaked Pink-Whistle, making the pig dance all round the mantelpiece as if it was angry. 'You stole me! You know you did! Take me back, take me back!'

'This is very strange,' said one of the men looking hard at Crooky. 'What does it mean?'

'Nothing. It's just a silly joke of some sort,' said Mr Crooky, beginning to tremble. 'I'll throw the pig into the dustbin.'

So he snatched it up, went into the yard and threw the pig hard into the dustbin. He slammed on the lid and went back to the house. How tiresome of this to happen just when he had called a meeting to ask his friends to give him money to start a shop! Now they might not trust him!

Pink-Whistle had gone into the yard with Mr Crooky. As soon as Crooky had gone back, Pink-Whistle took off the lid and fished out the pig. It was covered with tea leaves.

Pink-Whistle crept to the window. It was

open. To the men's enormous surprise, the money-box pig suddenly appeared on the window-sill, jigging and capering like mad, and a grunting voice could be heard at the same time. Then came the squeaky, piggy voice.

'You bad man! You put me in the dustbin! I'm covered with tea leaves – but you ought to be covered with shame! You stole me from those children. You know you did. Take me back, take me back!'

'This is most extraordinary and most disgraceful,' said one of the men, standing up. 'Mr Crooky, take that pig back at once. If you don't, I shall call the village policeman and ask him to listen to all the pig says.'

Mr Crooky felt as if he were in a bad dream. He stared at the pig, which turned a somersault and rattled like mad. 'I'm hungry!' it squeaked, 'I'm hungry. You put something into me, quick! I'm hungree-eeeeeeeeh!'

Mr Crooky felt so frightened that he put his hand into his pocket and pulled out all the money there. He popped it into the slit in the pig's back.

'More, more!' cried the pig, and Mr Crooky

put in more and more till he had no money left. 'Now take me home, home, home!' cried the pig, and leapt high into the air and back again to the window-sill. Mr Crooky thought that either he or the pig must be mad, or perhaps both of them. Or maybe it was a frightening kind of dream.

'Well, I'd better take you back, and then perhaps I shall wake up,' he said. So he snatched up the dancing pig, and ran off with it at top speed. He came to the children's garden and threw the pig over the wall. It landed on the grass.

Mr Crooky turned to go home. 'Now don't you *ever* do such a wicked thing again!' a voice boomed in his ear, making him almost jump out of his skin. It was Mr Pink-Whistle, of course, having one last go at Mr Crooky. The man tore off down the lane as if a hundred dogs were after him. Mr Pink-Whistle made himself visible and climbed over the wall into the garden. He called the children.

They came running to him and he showed them the pig, which he had picked up. 'Here you are,' he said. 'Safely back again – and heavier than before.'

The children shouted with delight. They

undid the little door in the pig's tummy and the money tumbled out. What a lot there was now!

'More than we ever put in!' cried Katie. 'Oh, how marvellous! How did it happen, little man? Tell us, do!'

But Pink-Whistle had vanished again. He didn't need to be thanked. It was enough to see the children's joyful faces, and to know that they could buy their mother the present they had saved up for – and could buy her something else besides now!

As for Mr Crooky, he didn't get the money lent to him for the shop he wanted to start – and a very good thing, too! He is still puzzled whenever he thinks of that grunting, dancing, talking pig, but if he happens to read this story, he won't be puzzled any more!

Chapter 7

Mr Pink-Whistle Has a Good Idea

One day Mr Pink-Whistle was going along down a quiet road, when he saw a face looking at him out of a window.

It was a nice face. It belonged to an old lady, whose hair shone silvery-grey in the sunshine, and whose eyes were blue and kind. But it was a sad face.

'I'll go by here tomorrow, and see if the old lady is still looking out,' thought Pink-Whistle. 'I shall be seeing that poor, old pony in the field at the bottom of this road every day for some time, so I can easily come down this road and look out for the old lady.'

Mr Pink-Whistle had made a new friend – a

very old pony, who had worked hard all his life, pulling heavy carts, and taking his master to market.

He would have been very happy if he had had a kind master, but the man he worked for was rough and impatient, too ready with the whip, and always shouting.

And now, when the pony was too old to pull heavy carts any more, and had been shut into the field, he was lonely and afraid.

'You see,' he said to Pink-Whistle, who, being half a brownie, understood animals very well, 'you see, Mr Pink-Whistle, I'm afraid that my master, now that I am no good to him, may sell me off to someone who will work me to death, and I really feel very tired and old now. I could do a little light work, but I'm afraid I couldn't do heavy work any more. I should fall down, and then I should be lashed and shouted at.'

'It's a shame,' said Pink-Whistle. 'It really is. But perhaps your master won't sell you to anyone who will work you like that. He certainly is not a kind or just man, but I don't believe his wife would let him do anything horrid to you.'

'He might even sell me to be killed and

sold as horse-flesh,' said the poor old pony. 'You see, I really am no use to him now! I might pull a baby's pram, but I couldn't pull a cart any more. Oh, Mr Pink-Whistle, I do feel so lonely and afraid sometimes. I don't know what I should do if you didn't come and talk to me.'

'Now I really can't bear this,' thought kind Pink-Whistle to himself, each time he left the old pony. 'What am I to do? I must put this right somehow, but how? Nobody wants a pony like that, and yet he deserves a little kindness and friendliness now, after having worked so hard and well all his life. It isn't fair.'

It wasn't fair. The farmer should have gone sometimes to the field, patted the old pony, and cheered him up. He should have told him that he could live out the rest of his days in peace and sunshine. But he didn't. He just grumbled because he couldn't get any more work out of him.

'If I could hear of anyone that wants an old pony like that I'd sell him,' he said to his wife. 'He's perfectly useless to me, but anyone with an old cart could still get a bit of work out of him.'

'Well, it's a good thing that there are so few horse-carts now,' said his wife. 'I'd hate you to sell old Brownie to a man who might whip him and try to make his poor old legs go faster than they can.'

Pink-Whistle thought a lot about the old pony. Anyone or anything in trouble made his kind heart very heavy and sad. And now he began to worry about the old lady who looked out of the window he passed every day.

'She looks so sad and lonely. She's got the same look in her eyes as the old pony. When people get old and tired they shouldn't be allowed to be sad and lonely.'

Every day he looked at the old lady and soon he began to smile and wave as he passed. She smiled back and waved, too. Each time Pink-Whistle went to see the old pony he kept a special smile for the old lady in the window.

Then one day he found some marigolds growing wild on a rubbish heap at the bottom of the field where the old pony lived. 'I'll take those to the old lady!' thought Pink-Whistle. So he picked them, made them into a nice little bunch, and that day, instead of passing the gate where the old lady lived, he opened it and marched up to the door!

But nobody opened it. A voice from the window said: 'I'm so sorry I can't open the door. I can't walk without help. Will you come to the window?'

So Pink-Whistle went to the window, beamed at the old lady, and gave her the marigolds. She put them into a glass of water and beamed back.

'How kind you are!' she said. 'I always look for your smile as you go down the street. Where do you go?'

Pink-Whistle told her about the old pony. The old woman listened with great interest.

'Poor old thing,' she said. 'Once I used to be rich and I had a pony-cart and pony of my own, and I used to drive about. Now I am poor, and somehow I have no friends. I am a poor, helpless old woman, no use to anyone – just like the old pony!'

'Can't you walk?' asked Pink-Whistle. 'If you could get about a bit you could soon make friends!'

'No, I can't walk,' said the old lady. 'There is something wrong with my legs. I did have a good friend who came in every day to take me out in my bath-chair – but now she has moved far away, and the woman who said she would come is cross and busy – too busy to take me out at all. She cleans my room for me, and helps me in and out of bed – but she can't spare the time to take me out.'

'So you never go out?' said Pink-Whistle. 'Well, well – what a pity! You must be very lonely and dull. I must come and see you sometimes.'

So he went to see her, and one day he pulled out the bath-chair from the cupboard it had stood in for months and managed to get the old lady tucked up in it. Then out they went – and the first thing Pink-Whistle did was to take her to see the old pony!

Well, you can guess how the two old things liked one another! The old lady had always loved horses – and the pony was delighted to find someone who knew how to talk to him, and click to him, and offer him a carrot. He nuzzled his brown head into her shoulder, and it was all Pink-Whistle could do to make them part.

One day the old lady was very excited. She had had a letter from her friend – and in it was some money!

'Look!' she said to Pink-Whistle. 'Money! But I don't want money at my age. So I am going to give it all to you, dear Mr Pink-Whistle, every bit – and you must buy a present for yourself from a grateful old lady. I don't know what I should have done without you.'

'I don't want your money,' said Pink-Whistle, smiling. 'You keep it and buy yourself a new shawl and a new armchair.

The old lady's eyes filled with tears. 'I don't want anything for myself,' she said. 'I did so want you to have the money, Mr Pink-Whistle. There is nothing I can do for you, nothing at all, in return for the happiness you have given to me – and I did think, I really did think this would be a little return for all your kindness.'

Pink-Whistle didn't know what to do. He felt as if he couldn't take money from the old lady – and yet she would be terribly unhappy if he didn't. After all, it *is* lovely to pay back kindness – and there was no other way she could do it.

And then a great idea came into Pink-

Whistle's head, and he grinned his wide grin. He held out his hand. 'I'll take the money,' he said, 'but on one condition, old friend – that I can do exactly as I like with it!'

'Of course you can,' said the old lady gladly, and gave him the money. Pink-Whistle trotted off quickly, full of his idea.

He went to the farmer who lived in his farmhouse beside the pony's field. He asked him how much the old pony was.

There was enough money to buy him. 'May I keep him in the field when he is not in use?' asked Pink-Whistle. The farmer said yes. Pink-Whistle trotted back to the old lady's house. He pulled out her bath-chair, and went off with it. She didn't see him, because she was asleep.

The little man took the chair to a leather-worker and asked him to fit it up so that it could be drawn along by a pony. 'That's easy,' said the man. 'You'll want reins, of course – and little shafts put here – and this bit altered there. I can do it in two days.'

'I'll help you, Dad,' said the man's small boy, a smiling, merry-eyed lad. ''Tisn't often we do a job like this, is it? I'd like to see a pony drawing this bath-chair. Is there a pony for it, Mister?'

'Yes,' said Pink-Whistle, and told the boy all about it. Then a good idea came to him. 'I suppose you wouldn't like to fetch the pony from the field every day to the old lady's house, and harness him to the bath-chair for her, would you?' he said. 'You're not very big and you could ride on the pony's back to and from the field.'

'Oooooh, yes,' said the small boy, his eyes shining with delight. 'I love horses, I'd just love that. Dad, may I do that?'

Pink-Whistle left the workshop, feeling very pleased. He had spent the old lady's money well! He had done something that would make the old pony very happy, for now he would have a friend, a nice light job of work – and a little boy to talk to him and even ride on his back a little each day. And the small boy would have some fun and feel quite important riding the pony, and harnessing him to the bath-chair each day.

'Well, it's wonderful what can be done if you really think hard enough,' said Pink-Whistle, trotting down the road very happily. 'I do wonder what the old lady will say!'

Well, you should have seen her face the

first day that the little boy came into the garden riding the old pony! Pink-Whistle arrived too, with the altered bath-chair. The little boy jumped down, and fitted straps and reins as his father had shown him. They both smiled and waved at the astonished old lady.

Then Pink-Whistle went into the house and helped the old lady to hobble slowly along to the bath-chair. She couldn't walk properly, she could only hobble a few steps. She got into the chair and Pink-Whistle tucked her up. He gave her the reins.

'Now, you said you know how to drive a horse,' he said. 'You needn't be afraid that the pony will go fast, because he won't. He's too old. He's so pleased to come and do a job of work like this for you. He's yours. I bought him with your money. Now – off you go!'

And off they went, the old lady driving the pony, and steering the bath-chair at the same time in a very clever way – but as the pony only walked slowly, there wasn't any danger of the old lady having an accident at all.

'Well, that's a fine sight to see, isn't it?' said Pink-Whistle, pleased, as he stared down the road after the two old friends, his hand on the small boy's shoulder. 'Now, you look out for them to come back – and take out the pony and ride him back to the field. Look after the old lady, too, and help her into the house.'

Good old Pink-Whistle! The old lady is as happy as she can be, driving out with her pony every day – and the old pony isn't afraid or lonely any more, because she is his friend. And he has the little boy, too, to talk to him and ride him carefully, and bring him a lump of sugar for a treat.

But the happiest of them all is Pink-Whistle, of course. 'There's nothing like putting bad things right,' he says. 'It's the finest thing anyone can do.'

I think so, too, don't you?

Chapter 8

Mr Pink-Whistle and the Eggs

Annabelle had five hens. Grandpa had given them to her on her last birthday, when they were quite small. Now they were big, and just beginning to lay.

Annabelle was delighted. 'Mummy, you shall have an egg for your breakfast every day!' she said. 'And so shall Daddy. And I will take two round to Granny and Grandpa every day, and there will be one egg for my breakfast, too. You will lay me five eggs, won't you, little red hens?'

The five hens looked at Annabelle and clucked. They liked this little girl who fed them each day, gave them fresh water, and cleaned out their house three times a week. They liked the way she talked to them, too. So they all clucked back, and Annabelle knew quite well what they said.

'They say they will certainly lay me five eggs every day,' she told her mother.

They did. Each morning when little Annabelle went to look in the nesting boxes there were five smooth brown eggs. Not very big ones, because the hens were young, but, oh, how delicious they tasted!

Daddy and Mummy had one each day. So did Annabelle. She took two round to Granny and Grandpa, always the biggest two, because it was Grandpa who had given her the little red hens.

And then one morning when Annabelle went to look for the eggs there was not a single one! All the nesting boxes were empty. What a shock for Annabelle. She stared at the empty boxes and then at the hens.

'Why haven't you laid me any eggs?' she said.

The hens clucked loudly. 'Cuck-cuck-cuck, we did, we did!' they said.

'You didn't,' said Annabelle. 'There aren't any at all. Please lay me some tomorrow.'

But there weren't any the next day either. Annabelle couldn't understand it. 'Perhaps someone is taking them,' she thought. 'Oh, dear, what a horrid thing to do.'

The next day there were no eggs again. Annabelle cried bitterly. 'It's a shame!' she said to the hens. 'I am sure somebody is stealing your eggs. It's a shame! You are my own hens, and you lay beautiful eggs that are mine – and now somebody else is taking them.'

A big black cat with green eyes was wandering by, not far from the hen-house. It stopped when it heard Annabelle crying, and listened to what she said.

Then it ran off quickly to its master. The cat was Sooty, Mr Pink-Whistle's own cat. She mewed for her master, and Mr Pink-Whistle came hurrying from the kitchen, where he was busy cleaning out his larder.

'A job for you to do, Master!' mewed Sooty. 'You leave the larder to me. I'll clean it all right! I've found a better job for you to do than that.'

'What is it?' asked Mr Pink-Whistle. 'Is it something I can put right? I haven't done a job like that for some time.'

'Yes, you can put it right, I expect,' said Sooty, and told Mr Pink-Whistle what had happened to Annabelle. 'She's such a dear little girl,' said Sooty. 'And somebody is really being very unkind, Master, to steal all her eggs.'

'I'll soon put that right!' said Mr Pink-Whistle, briskly. 'Where does she live? Oh, not very far away. That's good.'

Now, the next morning, just as it was beginning to get light, Mr Pink-Whistle went out. He made his way to Annabelle's house. Just as he turned in at her front gate he made himself invisible. Hey, presto! One moment he was there, and the next he was not. At least, he was, but nobody could see him.

He went down the garden to the hen-house. Scamp, the dog, heard him and smelt him, but couldn't see him. He growled a little in fright but didn't bark.

Mr Pink-Whistle went right to the bottom of the garden, where a tall hedge stood. Just beside it was the hen-house. Mr Pink-Whistle had a look round. Nobody about just yet. He opened the hen-house door and felt in the nesting boxes. Four eggs already – and a hen sitting in the fifth box!

He went out and shut the door softly. Then he stood on the path and waited in the dim light. He felt certain that the thief would soon be coming along, whoever he was.

Then very softy and silently, so that even Scamp's sharp ears heard no sound, somebody came through a gap in the hedge. Pink-Whistle looked at him. Dear, dear – who ever would have thought him to be the thief?

'It's Mr Smarmy,' said Pink-Whistle to himself. 'He goes to church. He sings hymns very loudly indeed. He always shakes his head and looks shocked when he hears of someone who has done wrong. And all the time he is taking little Annabelle's eggs!'

Mr Smarmy was well-dressed and neat. Even coming through the hedge had not made him untidy. He tiptoed to the hen-house, opened the door, and felt about for the eggs. One, two, three, four, five. Good! He put them carefully into his five pockets, and then went out. He backed through the hedge and pulled the branches together behind him. He was gone.

'So it's Mr Smarmy,' said Pink-Whistle again. 'I never did like him. Always so down on other people. Always finding fault with his gentle little wife. Always pretending to be so good and proper. Dear, dear – what a very horrid fellow, to be sure. I never did like deceitful people. Now what's to be done?'

Pink-Whistle went off to his own home. He went to his larder and looked in the egg-rack. There were six eggs there. He took five of them. He went back to the hen-house and popped them into the nesting boxes. 'Now Annabelle won't be disappointed!' he said. 'And tomorrow I'll play a nice little trick on Mr Smarmy.'

The eggs were white ones, not brown,

Annabelle was most astonished when she found them that morning. 'Look, Mummy!' she said. 'There are eggs this morning all right – but they are white, not brown. Isn't that strange?'

Now, that day Mr Pink-Whistle spent in a very peculiar way. He made five magic eggs, and how he chuckled as he made them. Sooty watched him and chuckled too.

Early the next morning Mr Pink-Whistle went along to Annabelle's hen-house again. There were five brown eggs there. He put them carefully into his pocket, and then put five magic eggs into the nesting-boxes instead. Then, quite invisible, he waited for Mr Smarmy to come along. The thief came silently through the hedge. He went into the hen-house and put the eggs carefully into his five pockets. Then he went out again.

Mr Pink-Whistle chuckled once more. He waited till Mr Smarmy had gone, then he popped back into the hen-house and put the brown eggs from his pocket into the nesting-boxes. Annabelle would find them there, quite safely.

Then he went home to breakfast. Sooty had got it ready for him. The big black cat laughed when she heard what her master had done.

'One of the magic eggs will go POP very loudly indeed,' said Mr Pink-Whistle. 'One will burst and make a very horrible smell. One will mew like a cat. One will cluck like a hen, and the last one will grow tiny legs and run all over Mr Smarmy.

Sooty giggled, and when a cat giggles it sounds very funny indeed. 'I wish I was going to see all that,' said Sooty.

'Well, I'm going to!' said Mr Pink-Whistle.

'I want to see Mr Smarmy taught a lesson. It's quite time he was!'

Now, Mr Smarmy, after he had taken the eggs, went to his sister Lucy's for breakfast. He didn't give her any of the eggs. Oh, no! He was going to take those home, after he had done his work that day, and ask his wife to make a nice fat omelette for him.

'I've got a busy day, Lucy,' he said. 'Got to see a lot of important people. Mustn't be late at the office. The first meeting is at half-past nine.'

Mr Smarmy arrived there at just before half-past nine. But he couldn't take any of the eggs out of his pockets because two of the men he was going to meet had already arrived.

'Good morning!' said Mr Smarmy. 'Nice and early! Aha! Here are the others, too!'

Soon seven men were sitting down round the table – and an eighth, who could not be seen, was standing opposite Mr Smarmy. That was Mr Pink-Whistle, of course, who had made himself invisible, and was at the meeting unknown to anyone.

The meeting began. Mr Smarmy wanted to ask the six men round him to lend him money for his business, so he was very polite indeed. Everyone listened to him quietly – till the first egg went POP.

'POP!' It burst with a loud noise, rather like a paper bag when it is blown up and goes bang. Everyone jumped and looked at Mr Smarmy. He looked alarmed. 'What was that?' he said.

'It sounded as if it came from somewhere about you,' said one man. 'Good gracious, look! What's that mess trickling out of one of your pockets? Looks like egg!'

It *was* egg, of course. Mr Smarmy looked down in disgust at the yellow mess that was seeping out of his pocket. How horrible! That egg must have been bad, to blow up like that!

He tried to wipe the mess away with his clean handkerchief. Then another egg began its magic work. It mewed like a cat!

'Mew-ew-ew-ew! Mew-ew-ew-ew!'

'There's a cat somewhere,' said one of the men. 'Sounds as if you've got it on your knee, Mr Smarmy.'

'Mew-ew-ew-ew!' Mr Smarmy jumped up in alarm, for the noise came from somewhere about him, there was no doubt of that. And then the mewing egg went off with a pop just as the other one had done!

Everyone jumped at the POP, and stared at another yellow mess coming from a pocket the other side of Mr Smarmy's coat. 'Is this some kind of a joke?' asked a man.

'No – no! I assure you I can't imagine *what* is happening!' said poor Mr Smarmy. 'Oh, dear – there goes another one!'

'POP!' Another egg burst, and this time there was such a terrible smell that everyone got out their handkerchiefs at once. 'Pooh,' said one of the men. 'Smarmy, do you often carry bad eggs about? I hope you are not a bad egg yourself! Pooh! What a fearful smell.'

Mr Smarmy was most distressed. This meeting was not going at all well. Blow those eggs! He wished he hadn't taken them that morning. They must all be bad ones. He heard a little chuckle close to his ear and turned in alarm.

It was Mr Pink-Whistle, but, of course, Mr Smarmy couldn't see him. Pink-Whistle was having a lovely time. What a joke! It was nice to see a horrid person like Mr Smarmy getting into trouble like this.

The meeting went on again, after Mr Smarmy had tried to clean himself up. And

then the fourth egg began to cluck like a hen.
It clucked very loudly indeed.

'Cuck-cuck-cuck-cuck-cuck! Cuck-cuck-cuck-
cuck-cuck! CUCK-CUCK!'

'Good gracious! He's got a hen in his
pocket now!' cried one of the men. 'Smarmy,
what is the meaning of this? Is this the way to
get us to lend money to you – to play idiotic
tricks of this kind?'

'Sir, I assure you –' began poor Mr Smarmy,
clutching in alarm at the egg that was
clucking, but before he could finish it went

POP, too! And then there was another yellow mess to clear up!

'Do you always carry bad eggs about with you?' asked one of the men. 'Have you any more? If so, I advise you to remove them from your pockets, Smarmy. We've had enough of eggs this morning.'

'There's one more,' said poor Smarmy, putting his hand into a pocket. 'I'll take it out. Oh – it's running away from me! Oh, it's gone down my trouser leg! Now it's running up again! It's inside my vest. It's tickling me. It's got legs, I'm sure.'

All the men stared at Mr Smarmy in amazement. The egg had grown legs, just as Pink-Whistle had said it would, and was running about all over him. He kept clutching at it, but it always slipped away somewhere else.

'He's mad!' said one of the men, getting up. 'Well, I didn't come here to have egg-tricks played on me. I'm not putting any money into a business run by a man who plays silly conjuring tricks with eggs that pop and mew and cluck and grow legs. Not I!'

'Nor I!' cried all the others, and they got up to go. Mr Smarmy stared at them in dismay.

'Please, please wait!' he cried. 'This is the last egg. Do wait!'

POP! The last egg burst, too – and that was enough for the men. They went out of the room, talking loudly about people who seemed to think it was funny to play tricks with bad eggs. Mr Smarmy was left alone, with a burst egg trickling down his leg.

He groaned. Then he felt a tap on his shoulder. He looked up in surprise, to see Mr Pink-Whistle looking sternly down at him. It made Mr Smarmy jump to see him there so suddenly.

'This is what happens to people who steal eggs from a little girl's hens,' said Mr Pink-Whistle. 'Bad things always come from bad deeds. None of those men will lend you the money you want. It serves you right.'

Mr Smarmy groaned again and buried his face in his hands. 'It does, I know it does,' he said. 'I'm a deceitful fellow. I pretend to be so good – and yet I am mean enough to take eggs belonging to a little girl's hens. I deserve all this. I don't know who you are, or how you know about it, or why those eggs behaved like that – I only know I'm ashamed and sorry.'

'That's good,' said Mr Pink-Whistle, pleased. 'Very good. What about buying a beautiful doll for the little girl, and putting it in the hen-house for her to find tomorrow, to make up for the eggs you took, Mr Smarmy? And what about trying to be as good and proper as you are always pretending to be? If you are really sorry, you can do that, too.'

And then away went Mr Pink-Whistle to tell Sooty all that had happened. But you may be sure he will be hiding, unseen, in the hen-house on the morning when there is a beautiful new doll waiting for Annabelle. She will be so surprised and pleased – and dear old Pink-Whistle wants to see her happy face.

He really is a kind old thing, isn't he?

Mr Pink-Whistle's Party

Mr Pink-Whistle's Party

Enid Blyton

Illustrations by Kevin Kimber

BLOOMSBURY
CHILDREN'S
BOOKS

Contents

1 Mr Pink-Whistle's Party   247

2 Mr Pink-Whistle at Work Again   260

3 Mr Pink-Whistle Comes Along   275

4 M. Pink-Whistle's Little Trick   289

5 Mr Pink-Whistle Gets a Letter   303

6 Well Done, Mr Pink-Whistle!   317

7 Mr Pink-Whistle and the Scribbler   330

8 Mr Pink-Whistle's Cat is Busy   341

Chapter 1

Mr Pink-Whistle's Party

You remember Mr Pink-Whistle, don't you – the little man with pointed ears who goes about the world putting wrong things right? He's half a brownie, and can make himself invisible if he wants to.

Mr Pink-Whistle often passed a little house called Merry-Chimneys. He liked that name – and he liked the little girl who lived there.

She always seemed to be swinging on her garden gate when he passed. She smiled at him and waved cheerily. One day he stopped and spoke to her.

'What's your name? It ought to be Smiley, because you're always smiling!'

The little girl laughed. 'Well, my name is *almost* as good as that,' she said. 'It's Merry.'

'Ah – Merry by name and merry by nature,' said Mr Pink-Whistle. 'Very nice. But do tell me – why are you so often out here swinging on your gate?'

'Oh, don't you know?' said the little girl. 'It's because there's a *"Please Cross Here"* sign.'

Mr Pink-Whistle looked surprised. He had certainly seen the *"Please Cross Here"* sign, and had noticed the thick white lines painted across the road, just opposite the little girl's house. But what had that got to do with swinging on a gate?

'You look puzzled!' said Merry. 'I'll explain.

Well, my mother says everyone ought to do something to help other people, and if we can't see something we've got to look for it. Mother said I'd got something right at the front gate – helping people over the busy crossing. Cars are supposed to stop, but they don't always.'

'Show me what you do,' said Mr Pink-Whistle.

'Well, look – there's a Toddlers' Home three doors away,' said Merry. 'And I'm waiting for the nurses to come out with the children, so that I can help them across the road. They have to wheel prams with four or five babies in them, so they can't very well look after the children who are walking, too. Here they come. Now watch.'

Merry skipped down from the gate and went to meet two nurses and a crowd of tiny children walking hand-in-hand in twos.

They were chattering like sparrows. The nurses had an enormous pram each with children in them. What a weight to push along!

'Hello, Merry. There's Merry! Merry, take my hand!' called the tiny children. The nurses nodded and smiled at the little girl, and went across the crossing with their prams. Merry carefully took every small child across herself, even holding up her hand to stop a car that was coming along.

When they had all gone over safely she skipped back to Mr Pink-Whistle. 'There you are,' she said. It's only a very little job, but it's a help, isn't it?'

'It certainly is,' said Mr Pink-Whistle. 'You did that well. Are you going in now you've done your job?'

'I've just got to wait for old Mr Lame and poor Mrs Limp,' said Merry. 'They come along about this time and somebody just has to help them across. They go so slowly, you see, and they are frightened of the cars. Here's Mr Lame.'

Pink-Whistle watched Merry guide the lame old fellow across the road. She chattered away to him, keeping a sharp eye out all the time for traffic. As soon as she got back to Pink-Whistle along came Mrs Limp. One of her legs was much shorter than the other, and she *really* couldn't hurry.

Merry took the limping woman safely across and carried her basket. Then she ran back again.

'Now I'm going in,' she said. 'I always know the time to come and swing on my gate and wait for all these people. Sometimes I come out just in case there might be somebody else afraid to cross – when I have a minute to spare. I suppose you wouldn't like me to help you across, would you?'

'I don't have to cross just here,' said Pink-Whistle. 'But thank you all the same. I'm glad to know you, Merry. There aren't many people like you in the world.'

The next time Mr Pink-Whistle passed by Merry's house, she waved to him again. 'Mr Pink-Whistle!' she called. 'Aren't I lucky! I'm going to a big party tomorrow, and I've got a new blue dress and blue shoes to match.'

'How lovely!' said Pink-Whistle. 'Well, you deserve a party, Merry.'

'There's going to be an enormous cake with candles,' said Merry. 'And a Punch and Judy Show – fancy that! And each child is to have two balloons and a present. Aren't I *lucky*!'

'I'll come by tomorrow morning at this time and you can show me your blue shoes,' said Mr Pink-Whistle. 'You get them out ready for me to see.'

But when he came the next day, there was no Merry swinging on the gate. He couldn't see her at all, not even at one of the windows. What could have happened?

'Perhaps she has gone shopping,' thought Pink-Whistle, and he waited a few minutes for her to come back. But she didn't. So Pink-Whistle walked up to the front door and rang the bell. A housekeeper answered the door and Pink-Whistle asked for Merry.

'She's out in the back garden,' said the

housekeeper. 'Would you like to go and find her?'

So out into the garden went Pink-Whistle and looked all round. There was a big lawn first, then an orchard, and then a kitchen garden. He couldn't see Merry anywhere. He walked down, puzzled.

No one was on the lawn. No one was in the orchard. Was anyone in the kitchen garden? No, there was nobody there, either.

There was a little garden shed nearby, and Mr Pink-Whistle thought he heard a noise coming from it – just a little noise. He went up and peeped in.

Yes. Merry was there – but what a different Merry! No smiles now, no merry laughter. She sat huddled up in a corner on an old sack, crying all by herself.

'What's the matter?' said Pink-Whistle, walking in and sitting down beside her.

'Oh, dear – you made me jump!' said Merry, wiping her eyes and giving him a very watery smile. 'Fancy you coming and finding me here!'

'Why aren't you out swinging on your gate as usual?' asked Pink-Whistle.

I'm not allowed to for three whole weeks,'

said Merry dismally. 'You see, I had a little friend to tea yesterday – and this morning her mother came to tell my mother that she's got measles. So I'm not allowed to swing on the front gate, or talk to any other children for three weeks, in case I get it too, and give it to someone else.

'That's very bad luck,' said Pink-Whistle. 'Very bad luck indeed. What about that party you were telling me of?'

'Well, of course, I can't possibly go to that,' said Merry, beginning to cry again. 'I'm sorry I'm so silly about it, but I just can't help feeling awfully disappointed. About my blue shoes and blue dress, you know – and not seeing the Punch and Judy Show. After all, I haven't been naughty or anything, have I? It isn't my fault.'

'It isn't – and you don't deserve such a disappointment,' said Pink-Whistle, comfortingly. 'But it just so happens that *I'm* giving a Punch and Judy party this afternoon, and *I'm* going to have an enormous cake with candles on, and there'll be balloons too – so you'll be able to come to that!'

Merry looked at him in astonishment. 'Are you *really* giving a party like that?' she said.

'But – I still won't be able to come, because I mustn't mix with other people.'

Oh, that's all right,' said Pink-Whistle, cheerfully. 'My guests can't get measles, so you can mix with them all you like. Shall we have the party down here in the orchard?'

'*Could* we? Because I'm not allowed to go anywhere by bus or train,' said Merry, her eyes beginning to shine. 'But why can't your guests get measles? I thought anybody could get them.'

'Not *my* guests,' said Pink-Whistle, getting up. 'Well, put on your blue shoes and your blue dress this afternoon, and be here at three o'clock. Don't forget.'

He went off, leaving the little girl in such a state of excitement that she danced round every tree in the orchard. What a funny, wonderful little man Mr Pink-Whistle is!'

At three o'clock, dressed in her blue shoes and blue dress, with a blue ribbon in her hair, Merry ran down to the orchard. Good gracious me! What had happened to it!

Every tree was hung with streamers and shining ornaments. Great big toadstools had sprung up from the grass for tables and seats. Twelve had grown close together to make an extra big table for the guests to sit at.

The guests were coming from every direction. But they weren't children. Oh no – Mr Pink-Whistle had chosen his other kind of friends – the pixies and elves and brownies. There they came, trooping along, all dressed in their best, too!

Mr Pink-Whistle was welcoming them all, smiling even more broadly than usual. He saw Merry and went up to her. 'You look lovely in your blue shoes and blue dress,' he said. 'I'm so glad you could come to my party. Now let me tell you who's here. This is Tiptoe – and this is Jinky – and this is Silky – and this is Jolly – and this is Heyho – dear me, I hope you'll remember all their names!'

Merry liked all the little people at once. She played games with them, ate the ice-creams that kept appearing on the little mushroom tables, and drank glasses of honey-lemonade. Lovely!

The tea was simply glorious. Merry counted twelve different kinds of most extraordinary sandwiches, and twelve different kinds of cakes. There were wobbly jellies and fruit salads with ice-cream on top. And oh, the cake, the cake that stood in the middle of the big table!

It shone and glittered with a hundred coloured candles, and it was decorated with silver and gold balls, pink, yellow and white icing, and all kinds of sugared flowers that could be eaten.

'See what's written on the top, Merry,' said Pink-Whistle. Merry looked and went red with pleasure.

'WELCOME TO MERRY!' was written in pink icing.

'Yes, it's *your* cake,' said Pink-Whistle. 'Made specially for you. Now – what about cutting it?'

After tea there was a Punch and Judy Show. It was much better than any show Merry had ever seen, and she laughed so much that she got a stitch.

Everyone had two balloons. 'They won't burst,' said Pink-Whistle. 'They've got just a touch of magic in them. They'll last for years.'

It was the loveliest party Merry had ever been to. At the end every guest had a present in a little shiny box. They all lined up and went to Pink-Whistle one by one.

'Thank you, Mr Pink-Whistle,' each little guest said. 'Thank you for having me to your lovely party. Goodbye!'

Merry said the same – and she gave the kind little man a sudden hug. 'You planned your party for *me*, I know you did!' she said. 'It's the nicest one I've ever been to. I love you, Mr Pink-Whistle. You go round the world putting things right – and that's what *I'm* going to do too!'

'You do it already – that's why I gave this party for you,' said Pink-Whistle. Well, good-bye, and I hope you'll like your present. I'll

look out for you on the gate in three weeks'
time!'

Merry opened her parcel when she got
indoors. You will never guess what was inside!
Very neatly folded, wrapped carefully in
tissue paper, was – a pair of silvery wings!
There was a little note tied to them.

'These can be fitted on your shoulders and
used on every full-moon night. Please put
away carefully when not in use.'

'What a present!' said Merry, softly, in the
greatest delight. 'Wings! Wings of my own!'
She shook them out gently, and looked at the
calendar on the wall.

'Oh, dear – it won't be a full-moon night
for ten days! How can I possibly wait?'

She'll have to wait, of course – but won't
she be pleased to go flying in the garden
when the moon is big and round and shiny!
Dear old Pink-Whistle – he does know how to
make people happy, doesn't he?

Chapter 2

Mr Pink-Whistle at Work Again

One day, when Mr Pink-Whistle was sitting eating an egg for his breakfast, his pointed ears heard something far away. Sooty, his cat, looked at him. She could hear something, too.

'It's somebody crying,' said Mr Pink-Whistle, getting up in a hurry. 'It sounds like a child. I haven't time to finish my toast, Sooty. I'll be back soon, I hope.'

Mr Pink-Whistle hurried to put on his hat, and then went down the garden path at top speed. He could still hear that crying.

He hopped on a bus, and went for some way, and then hopped off again. He stood and listened, his pointed ears moving like a dog's. Ah – the crying was somewhere over there – somewhere near that cottage.

Off he went, stepping softly, and soon he came to where a little girl was sitting, leaning against an old wall. She wasn't crying very loudly, as you might have thought because of Mr Pink-Whistle hearing her so far away, but quite softly.

'What's the matter?' asked Mr Pink-Whistle. The little girl looked up. She wasn't at all afraid to see Mr Pink-Whistle, his green eyes were so kind.

'Oh – did you hear me crying?' she said. 'I thought I was being very quiet.'

'Yes. I heard you,' said Mr Pink-Whistle, and he sat down beside her. 'Now – what's the matter? I'm Mr Pink-Whistle, and I try to put wrong things right. Maybe I can put something right for you?'

'Oh – are you really Mr Pink-Whistle?' said the little girl, in delight. 'I've read about you, and I always wanted to meet you. But I'm afraid you can't put things right for *me*.'

'You tell me, and I'll see,' said Pink-Whistle, and he took out a big bag of peppermints. 'Let's have one of these while we talk.'

'Well, it's like this,' said the little girl, taking a peppermint. 'I haven't got a father or mother, so my auntie looks after me. She's not very fond of me, really, because she thinks it's a nuisance to have me to see to. But she's all I've got. And now she's getting married and going out to Canada – so, of course, she doesn't want me any more – and – and –'

'And you're going to be sent away to strangers, and you're afraid,' said Mr Pink-Whistle at once. 'Here, take my hanky – it's bigger than yours and cleaner.'

The little girl rubbed her face with Pink-Whistle's hanky, and tried to stop crying. 'Yes,

I'm to go to somebody called Mrs Clamp, and she's got three boys all bigger than me, and a little girl who doesn't want me there. Mrs Clamp scolds people a lot, and I'm frightened.'

'What you want is somebody to love you, isn't it? said Mr Pink-Whistle. 'A real mother?'

'Oh, yes – wouldn't that be lovely!' said the little girl, beaming. 'You know – the kind of mother who welcomes you home from school and wants to know what you've been doing, and looks after you when you're not well, and makes you a cake on your birthday, and fills your stocking at Christmas, and says good-night to you when you're in bed.'

'I know the kind of mother you mean,' said Mr Pink-Whistle. 'It's the kind of mother most children have. Dear, dear – what a pity that a nice little girl like you can't make some mother very happy.'

'I'd try my hardest,' said the little girl earnestly. 'But mothers all have children of their own and they don't want me. I suppose, Mr Pink-Whistle – I suppose you don't know any children who don't want their mother and would let me have her?'

'I know plenty of children who aren't good

or kind to their mothers,' said Mr Pink-Whistle, handing out another peppermint, 'but that doesn't really mean they want to give her away! This is a difficult problem, little girl. By the way, what is your name?'

'Alice,' said the little girl. She gave Pink-Whistle back his hanky. 'I'm all right now,' she said. 'It's nice to have you for a friend, Mr Pink-Whistle. I don't wonder that all the children love you.'

'Well, well – that's a nice thing to say,' said Pink-Whistle, pleased. 'Look here – I can't think what to do about you – but do you think your aunt would let you come and stay with Sooty – that's my cat – and me, for a day or two, whilst I look round? Has she heard of me?'

'Oh, yes,' said Alice. 'Sometimes she's read me stories about you, so she knows you already.'

Well, that's how it happened that Mr Pink-Whistle had little Alice to stay with him. Sooty was delighted. The little girl was so kind and willing. She wanted to do all kinds of jobs for Pink-Whistle, and you should just have seen how well she darned his socks, and mended a hole in his shirt!

She was sweet to Sooty, too, and helped her to clean the house, and even brushed the fur on top of her head, where Sooty couldn't reach to lick.

Mr Pink-Whistle couldn't seem to find anyone who would be a good mother to Alice. They all seemed so busy and worried and tired. It would never do to ask them to look after yet another child.

He talked to Sooty about it and Sooty had an idea.

'You know, Master,' she said, 'there's Miss Trot-About in the next village. She lives in Cherry Cottage, and –'

'Yes, I remember her,' said Pink-Whistle. 'Isn't she the one with five cats and a parrot?'

'Yes,' said Sooty. 'That's how I know so much about her. I know all the cats, you see. They say Miss Trot-About is the kindest, nicest person, who never forgets their fish and milk, and –'

'Yes, yes,' said Pink-Whistle, 'but if she's got all those cats to fuss about, surely she wouldn't want a little girl?'

'I think it's because she hasn't got a little girl or boy that she fusses over the cats,' said Sooty. 'She's the kind of person that's got to love somebody, you see, somebody of her own. Well those cats are hers, and she really does love them.'

'It's an idea,' said Pink-Whistle, thinking hard. 'Yes, it really is.'

He went over to see Miss Trot-About. She was feeding all her cats. He noticed that she was limping and walking with a stick.

'Good morning, Mr Pink-Whistle,' she said. 'Excuse my limping like this. I've got a very bad leg, and I really ought to be in bed for a bit – but there's nobody I can trust to see to my pussies.'

'Well!' said Mr Pink-Whistle at once, 'I wonder if you'd like a little friend of mine to come and see to them for you. She's staying with me now, and Sooty, my cat, loves her. She would be very pleased to come and look after both you and your cats, I'm sure. And the parrot, too.'

'Really?' said Miss Trot-About. 'Well, if she's a friend of *yours*, Mr Pink-Whistle, she must be all right. Bring her over. But mind – if I don't like her, back she comes the very next day!'

'Certainly, certainly,' said Pink-Whistle, and off he went, all the cats following him to the gate. He whistled gaily as he caught the bus home. Had he managed to put a wrong thing right again? He would soon know.

He told Alice about poor Miss Trot-About and her bad leg, and all her cats and the parrot. Alice listened hard.

'She ought to be in bed for a little while,' she said. 'Mr Pink-Whistle, should I just pop over there for a day, and let her have a rest? I'm sure I could look after the cats – and the parrot, too.'

'Well, that certainly would be kind,' said

Pink-Whistle. And that's how it came about that Alice went over to stay with Miss Trot-About till her leg got better.

Miss Trot-About had only two bedrooms, her own and a little one under the eaves. It had a slanting roof, and a climbing rose looked in at the window. A small bed stood by the wall. Alice looked at the room in delight.

'Oh – am I going to sleep here?' she said. 'Oh, Miss Trot-About, I do love your house. It's a *home*, isn't it, not just a house. You've so many flowers about, and I like your bright cushions, and your clock has such a nice loud tick, and isn't it lovely the way the cats all curl up in their own baskets.'

'Dear me – what a long speech,' said Miss Trot-About, pleased. 'Now, do you think you can cook the fish for the cats, and give them their meal? And the parrot's cage wants cleaning out, and –'

'Oh, Miss Trot-About, of course I can do all that!' said Alice. 'I'd love to. But won't you get into bed and rest your leg? That's why I've come, you know – to look after things for you till your leg's better! The cats will be all right – see how they follow me about already!'

Well, Alice settled into that little cottage as

if she had lived there all her life. The cats loved her. The parrot talked to her all day long. Even the hens out in the garden came clucking when she called them.

Miss Trot-About stayed in bed for two days – then another day – and then another and another. She heard Alice trotting round, humming, talking to the parrot, fussing the cats, lighting the gas under the kettle, and generally sounding as happy as could be.

'I must get up tomorrow,' said Miss Trot-About each day. But she didn't. 'Oh, dear, I can't,' she said to herself. 'My leg is quite better. I'm a fraud, I know. But if I get up and show that I'm better, little Alice will go. I can't bear her to go. She's better than the cats, and a hundred times nicer than the parrot. If ever I'd had a little girl I would have wanted one just like Alice!'

Well, of course, Miss Trot-About had to get up at last! She got up really because Mr Pink-Whistle called to say he was coming to tea that day. That meant he would take Alice away. Alice watched her coming quite easily downstairs.

'Oh – your leg really and truly is better!' she said. 'I'm so glad!'

'Oh, *dear*!' thought Miss Trot-About, 'she's glad I'm better so that she can go. I expect she's bored being here so long, poor child. Well, she really has been very good. I must give her a nice present.'

Miss Trot-About took hardly any notice of her cats! She didn't even speak to her parrot. She talked to Alice all the time, and fetched a little blue skirt she thought she could make into a dress for her, and asked her what her favourite cake was so that she could make it for tea.

Alice suddenly ran to her and gave her a hug. 'Do you know,' she said, 'you're *just* like a mother!'

Miss Trot-About was so surprised that she couldn't say a word. Well, well – that was about the very nicest thing anyone had ever said to her in her life. Just like a mother! Would you believe it?

Mr Pink-Whistle came to tea. He hadn't been near Alice and Miss Trot-About since he had left Alice at the cottage. He badly wanted to know what had happened. Did Miss Trot-About like Alice? Did Alice want to stay? Would they tell him some good news?

But they didn't. Miss Trot-About was sure

that Pink-Whistle had come to fetch Alice, and she was sure that Alice wanted to go.

And Alice was sure that Pink-Whistle was going to take her away, and perhaps send her to Mrs Clamp, and she was sure that Miss Trot-About wouldn't want her any longer now that she was better.

'Well – did you have a happy time together?' said Mr Pink-Whistle at last.

'Oh, very,' said Miss Trot-About. 'But I'm sure Alice is ready to go now.'

'A very, very happy time,' said Alice, 'but I'm sure Miss Trot-About will be glad to be on her own again.'

Mr Pink-Whistle sighed. What a pity! This was something he hadn't managed to put right after all.

'You'd better get your little bag,' he said to Alice. 'It's time we went. What a lovely tea that was, Miss Trot-About. Thank you very much.'

He went to help Alice with her bag. She was in her dear little room, tears in her eyes. 'I hate to say goodbye to it, Mr Pink-Whistle,' she said. 'It's so homely. And Miss Trot-About is just like a real mother. I do love her. I just hate to go. If only she would love me instead of her cats!'

'Now you just stay here a minute and dry your eyes,' said Pink-Whistle, taking her bag. 'Don't let Miss Trot-About see you crying. It would upset her.'

He went down with the bag and popped his head round the sitting-room door. 'Just going,' he said, and then he stopped in surprise. Miss Trot-About was dabbing her eyes with her hanky!

'Well – what's the matter with you?' said Pink-Whistle, quite expecting the parrot to burst into tears next.

'Nothing. Nothing, really,' said Miss Trot-

About. 'It's just that I shall miss Alice so dreadfully, and I'm such a fraud, Mr Pink-Whistle. My leg was better days ago, but I wouldn't get up because I wanted to keep Alice to the very last minute. I wish I was her mother. She's just exactly right for me. She's much better than five cats and a parrot. I do so wish she was mine!'

Alice came in just as Miss Trot-About said all this. She listened in the greatest surprise. Then she flew over to Miss Trot-About and put her arms round her.

'I heard you! Well, if you wish you were my mother, so do I! I won't leave you! Don't let me go, don't let Mr Pink-Whistle take me away!'

'I won't. He shan't,' said Miss Trot-About, suddenly looking so very fierce that Mr Pink-Whistle backed away in alarm.

'Go away, Mr Pink-Whistle,' said Miss Trot-About. 'I shan't allow you to take Alice away. This is her home. I won't allow you to send her to Mrs Clamp. What a very wicked thing to do!'

'And I won't leave Miss Trot-About,' said Alice. 'It's no good, Mr Pink-Whistle, I just won't come with you. I'm needed here. We love each other, and no matter *what* you say I'm going to live here with Miss Trot-About. So there!'

They both looked so fierce that Pink-Whistle hardly dared to say a word. He just said, 'Goodbye, bless you both,' and disappeared out of the door.

When he had gone, Miss Trot-About and Alice looked at one another. 'Do you know – I have a feeling that Mr Pink-Whistle meant this to happen?' said Miss Trot-About. 'He was just putting another wrong thing right. He didn't *want* to take you away. And instead of thanking him, we've been cross. Oh, dear!'

'Never mind. He'll understand,' said Alice. 'We'll ask him to tea again on Friday – and we'll have the most wonderful cake you ever saw, with "Thank you, Mr Pink-Whistle" on top of it. He's a darling.'

He is, of course – and I can just imagine how pleased he will be when he sees that cake, can't you?

Chapter 3

Mr Pink-Whistle Comes Along

'Sooty!' called Mr Pink-Whistle to his big black cat, 'I'm going out for a walk. It's a lovely, sunny winter's day. I'll be back in time for dinner.'

Sooty went to the door to see him off. He went briskly down the garden path and out of the gate. The frost crunched under his feet as he went, and the pale December sun shone down on him. What a lovely day!

'I think I'll go down to the pond and see if there are any children sliding on it,' he thought. So off he went, down the lane, up the hill, down the hill, and across a meadow where frost whitened the long grass in the ditches.

Mr Pink-Whistle was just putting his leg

over the stile to go to the pond when his sharp ears heard a sound. He had pointed brownie ears and could hear like a hare!

'Now, what's that?' he thought, a leg half over the stile. 'Is it an animal? Or a child? Or just a noise?'

It seemed to come from a little tumble-down shed by the hedge. Mr Pink-Whistle listened. Yes, there certainly was a noise – a sniffy sort of noise – sniff-sniff-gulp, sniff-sniff!

'I'd better go and find out,' said Pink-Whistle, and he got down from the stile and went to the little shed. He poked his head inside. It was rather dark and he couldn't see anything at first. Then he saw something white. 'Dear me!' said Pink-Whistle. 'Is that a face I see? Does it belong to someone? Who are you?'

The face was peeping out of a pile of hay in the corner. It spoke.

'Yes, but please go away. This is *my* shed. It's private.'

Pink-Whistle didn't go away. He was sure that he could see that the face was very miserable. He came right into the shed.

Somebody scrambled out of the hay,

crossly. It was a boy of about ten. 'I told you this was *my* shed,' he said. 'It's on my father's land and he said I could have it for my own. You're trespassing!'

'Was it you I heard sniff-sniff-sniffing?' asked Pink-Whistle. 'What's the matter?'

'Nothing,' said the boy. 'Nothing to do with you anyway. Don't you know when people want to be alone? I wish you'd get out of my shed.'

'I'm going,' said Pink-Whistle. 'But it's a pity you haven't even a dog to keep you company. If you're unhappy, it's nice to have a dog's nose on your knee.'

He walked to the door. 'Come back,' said the boy suddenly, in a shaky sort of voice. 'I like what you said just now. You might understand if I tell you something. You wouldn't have said that if you hadn't understood what friends dogs are, would you?'

'No,' said Pink-Whistle, turning back. 'So it's something to do with a dog, is it? Your own dog, I suppose.'

'Yes,' said the boy, sitting down on the hay and rubbing a very dirty hand over his face. 'You see, I've got no brothers or sisters, so my dad gave me a dog for my own. My very own, you understand – not one that's shared by the whole family. Buddy was my own, every whisker of him, every hair.'

'That's a fine thing,' said Pink-Whistle. 'I expect that you belonged to him as much as he belonged to you. You were his friend as much as he was yours.'

'I'm glad you understand,' said the boy.

'It's nice to tell somebody. Well, Buddy's gone. Somebody's stolen him. He was a golden spaniel with big, loving eyes, and he cost my father a lot of money. That's why he's been stolen, because he's valuable.'

Sniff-sniff-sniff! The boy rubbed his hand over his eyes again. 'I'm ten,' he said, ashamed, 'and too old to make a fuss like this, like a four-year-old. I know all that, so you needn't tell me. But a dog sort of gets right into your heart if he's your own.'

'I shall begin to sniff, too, in a minute!' said Pink-Whistle. 'I know exactly what you feel. You're thinking how miserable your dog will be without you, and you're hoping that nobody is being cruel to him, and you're wondering if he's cowering down in some corner, puzzled and frightened. Well, that's enough to make anyone feel miserable.'

'He disappeared yesterday,' said the boy. 'Two men came to the farm to ask if they could buy chickens – and I'm sure they took Buddy away. They may have given him some meat with a sleeping-powder in it and got him like that. I don't know. The police say they can't trace the men and they haven't had any report of a golden spaniel anywhere.'

'I see,' said Pink-Whistle. 'Er – do you happen to know me by any chance, boy?'

'My name's Robin,' said the boy. 'No – I don't know you. I've never ever seen you before, have I?'

He peered closely at Pink-Whistle. The sun shone in at the little shed window just then and he suddenly saw Pink-Whistle clearly. He saw his green eyes and pointed ears, and he gave a little cry.

'Wait! Wait! Yes, I've seen your picture somewhere in a magazine or a book. Yes, I remember now. Why – surely you're not Mr Pink-Whistle?'

'I am,' said Pink-Whistle, beaming all over his face, pleased that the boy knew him. 'And I like to go about the world putting wrong things right.'

'Get back Buddy for me then, please, *please*!' said Robin, clutching hold of Mr Pink-Whistle's arm. 'I never thought you were real, but you are. Can you get back Buddy?'

'I'll do my best,' said Pink-Whistle. 'I'll go now. Cheer up, get out of this dark shed and go home and find some work to do. Perhaps I can put things right for you.'

He walked out of the shed. Robin ran after

him, suddenly very cheerful indeed. He was amazed. To think that Mr Pink-Whistle should have come along just then – what a wonderful thing!

Pink-Whistle went back home. He called Sooty, his cat, and told her about Robin. 'Go to the farm and speak to the farm cats,' he said. 'They will have noticed these two men and have seen if Buddy was taken away by them. Find out all you can.'

Sooty ran off, tail in the air. She soon came back with news. 'Yes, Master! The farm cats say that the men came back that evening, threw down meat for Buddy and then went away. Buddy ate it and fell asleep. Then the men came back and put him into a sack. They had a wagon drawn by a horse called Rip, who told the cats that his masters went to Ringdown Market every Thursday. You will find them there.'

'Thank you, Sooty,' said Pink-Whistle. 'That's all I want to know.'

The next day was Thursday. Pink-Whistle set off to Ringdown Market. It was a long way away, but he got there at last. What a babble of sound there was! Horses whinnying, sheep baaing, hens clucking, ducks quacking, turkeys gobbling, geese hissing and cackling!

Pink-Whistle looked for a golden spaniel. There were three for sale at the market. Which was Robin's? Mr Pink-Whistle decided to make himself invisible. This was a gift he sometimes used, and he used it now!

One moment there was a kindly man walking about – the next moment he wasn't there at all! An old woman selling eggs was most astonished. She blinked her eyes in wonder and then forgot about it. Pink-Whistle went up to a golden spaniel. 'Buddy!' he whispered. 'Buddy!'

The dog took no notice. So that one wasn't Robin's dog. Pink-Whistle went up to the second spaniel and whispered. But he wasn't Robin's dog either.

'Buddy!' whispered Pink-Whistle to the third spaniel, who was lying miserably on some sacks behind two men selling hens. 'Buddy!'

The dog sprang up at once, his tail wagging. He looked all round. Who had called him by his name? One of the men turned round sharply.

'Lie down, you!' he said, and kicked him. Pink-Whistle felt very angry indeed. Ah!

These fellows wanted punishing. They
wanted frightening. Well, he would have a
fine game and give them a wonderful
punishment.

He began to bark like a dog and Buddy
pricked up his ears at once. Then Pink-
Whistle pretended that Buddy was speaking.

'Hens, peck these men!' he cried. And then
it seemed to the men as if a whole flock of
invisible hens were all round them, pecking
hard – but really, of course, it was Mr Pink-
Whistle jabbing at them with his hard little
forefinger – peck-peck-peck!

The men cowered back, squealing. Everyone came to see what the matter was. Pink-Whistle began to cluck and that made the men think there really were invisible hens pecking them.

Then Pink-Whistle called out again in a barking sort of voice, so that it seemed as if Buddy was talking: 'Geese, attack these men!'

And dear me, what a cackling there was from old Pink-Whistle then, what a hissing – and what a jab-jab-jabbing from top to bottom of the scared men. Everyone stared, amazed. *What* was happening? Where did the cackling and hissing come from? Who was jabbing at the men?

'Serves them right,' said somebody. 'I never did like those two.'

And then, oh dear, Pink-Whistle decided to be a butting goat! What fun he was having – and what a wonderful punishment he was giving the two men!

'Goat, butt them!' he cried, and the men looked everywhere, scared, wondering if an invisible goat was coming at them.

Biff! Pink-Whistle ran first at one man and then at another. Biff! Bang! Biff! The men felt exactly as though a big, rather solid goat was butting them back and front. Pink-Whistle butted one man right over and he rolled on top of Buddy. Buddy promptly snapped at him and growled.

Pink-Whistle immediately growled too, and talked in his growling. 'Bull, toss these men!'

The men gave a loud howl. Hens had pecked them, geese had jabbed them, a goat had butted them! Surely, surely they were not going to be tossed by a bull, and an invisible one, too, coming at them from any side!

'Run for it!' yelled one man, and he ran for his life. The other followed. Pink-Whistle galloped after them, making his feet sound like a bull's hooves – clippitty-clippitty-clop. How the men howled!

Pink-Whistle couldn't follow them very far because he laughed so much. How he laughed! People were really very puzzled to hear loud chuckles and not to see any one there.

'Well, I don't know what's upset those two fellows,' said a burly farmer, 'but I'm glad to see the back of them. Rascals, both of them!'

Pink-Whistle went back to where the dog Buddy lay on the sacks, puzzled and frightened. Buddy suddenly heard a quiet, kindly voice talking to him, and invisible fingers undid the knot of rope that tied him to a rail.

'Come with me, Buddy,' said the voice, and Buddy went obediently. He sniffed at Mr Pink-Whistle's invisible legs. How very peculiar to smell legs that didn't seem to be there! Buddy couldn't understand it – but then, he didn't really understand anything that had happened since he had left Robin. His world seemed quite upside-down and not at all a nice place.

It was a long way to the farm where Robin lived – but as they got nearer to it Buddy became very excited indeed. His nose twitched. He pulled against the hand on his collar.

'Not so fast, Buddy,' said Mr Pink-Whistle. 'I want to come with you.'

Buddy took another sniff at the invisible legs. Well, they smelt all right, so the person with them ought to be all right, too. He trotted along obediently, getting more and more excited.

It was dark when at last they came to the farm. Buddy was now so excited that he pulled and pulled at Pink-Whistle's hand.

The little man led him to his kennel. 'Get in there and wait,' he ordered. 'And bark. Bark loudly!'

Buddy crept in and then he barked. How loudly he barked. 'Wuff-wuff-wuff, WUFF-WUFF. Robin, I'm back, where are you? WUFF-WUFF!'

And Robin heard, of course. He would know Buddy's bark anywhere! He sprang up at once, his face shining. 'Mother! That's Buddy's bark! He's back!' he cried, and raced

287

out of the house to the yard. He came to the kennel, calling joyfully.

'Buddy! BUDDY! I'm here!'

And, before Buddy could squeeze past the invisible Mr Pink-Whistle, there was Robin, squeezing into the kennel! He got right in, and then you really couldn't tell which was boy and which was dog, they hugged and licked and rolled and patted, and yelped and shouted so joyfully together!

At last, tired out, they sat peacefully together in the kennel. Buddy's nose on Robin's knee and Robin's arm round Buddy's neck. Only Buddy's tongue was busy, lick-lick-licking at Robin's hand.

'Buddy! I do wish I could say a big thank you to Mr Pink-Whistle!' said Robin. 'I don't even know where he lives, though. I'd say, Mr Pink-Whistle, I'm your friend for ever and ever!'

Pink-Whistle heard it all. He was peering in at the kennel, as happy as could be. He had put a lot of wrong things right in his life, but surely this was one of the very best! He stole away in the darkness, a very happy little man indeed.

Chapter 4

Mr Pink-Whistle's Little Trick

One winter's afternoon, just as it was getting dark, Mr Pink-Whistle walked down a road near a school.

'Let me see – it's just about the time that the children come out of afternoon school,' said Mr Pink-Whistle, trying to see the time by his watch. 'I'll watch them as they go by. Perhaps one or two of them will know me!'

So he stood by a shop and waited. Soon he heard chattering and clattering – and out came all the children from the school down the road.

Two small girls came first, talking together. They walked along and didn't notice Pink-Whistle. Just as they had passed him, another child ran up – a big boy. As he passed the two little girls he swerved and bumped into them both.

Down went one of them – and the other was sent into the nearby wall. They screamed.

The boy roared with laughter and ran on. 'It's Sam again!' said one girl, picking herself up. 'Horrid thing – why does he always have to bump into people when he passes them? I suppose he thinks it's funny.'

'Your coat is all muddy,' said the other little girl. 'Your mother will be awfully cross! How I hate Sam! He's always so rough.'

Mr Pink-Whistle was just going to go up to the two children to see if he could do anything about the little girl's coat when they ran off together. He frowned. What a horrible boy! Did he really make a habit of bumping into others like that?

A small boy came by with his satchel on his back – and suddenly someone swooped down on him, bumped into him and knocked him flying!

'You beast, Sam!' yelled the small boy. 'Lying in wait for me again! I'll tell my father.'

'Pooh!' shouted back Sam, and shot off across the road. Mr Pink-Whistle went to help the small boy to pick up his books. They were lying in a puddle.

'Oh – thanks,' said the boy. 'Gosh, I shall get into a row – all my books soaked! Blow Sam! I bet he's hiding somewhere near to bump into as many of us as he can. He's so big, you see – the biggest of our class.'

It was rather dark now and the little boy couldn't see Pink-Whistle clearly. How pleased he would have been if he had known who it was that was helping him!

A girl came along after that, and two more behind her. Pink-Whistle stood nearby, watching out for the horrid Sam. Was he hiding somewhere again so that he could rush out at these children, too?

Yes – he was! Whoosh! He shot across the road and bumped heavily into the first little girl – and then swung round to bump into the others. Pink-Whistle shouted a warning to them.

'Hey – look out!'

They just got out of Sam's way in time and he almost crashed into the wall himself. He peered into the shadows angrily, trying to see who it was that had warned the two girls. He was afraid that it might be a policeman, and he shot off into the darkness.

Pink-Whistle felt sure that he wouldn't appear again, and he set off down the street, wondering if he could do anything about this tiresome Sam.

Suddenly someone came running behind him, and bumped hard into him, giving him a shove at the same time. A shout of laughter told Mr Pink-Whistle that it was Sam again!

Over went the little man like a skittle – Sam was certainly good at bumping! Pink-Whistle found himself sitting in a big patch of soft mud – most unpleasant!

'Ha! Sam again, I suppose!' he said, angrily. 'I'm small – so he thought I was a child. Well, it's certainly time he was stopped – and I'll soon stop him, too!'

Pink-Whistle got up, caught a bus and went home to his little cottage. He told Sooty, his cat, all that had happened. Sooty grinned. She put Pink-Whistle's coat to dry, and made him some tea.

'You want to get the old Wobbly-Man to walk down the street,' she said. 'It would give Sam a most unpleasant surprise to find someone he couldn't possibly push over!'

'Good idea,' said Pink-Whistle. 'And what about me walking down the pavement carrying a nice bunch of prickly holly, Sooty?'

'I'd like to be there and see Sam bumping into that!' said Sooty. 'And what about putting a hat and a pair of boots and a coat on a great big balloon, and putting a walking spell into the boots?'

Pink-Whistle nearly fell off his chair with laughing. 'Oh dear – you do think of peculiar things,' he said to Sooty. 'Yes, we'll certainly do the balloon idea. You see, it's just too dark to see properly at that time in the afternoon – so Sam won't be able to see who he's bumping, and as I and the Wobbly-Man are both small, he will think we are children and become rushing full speed at us!'

'And he's sure to want to bump into someone who looks nice and fat like the Walking Balloon,' said Sooty. 'Well, you're certainly going to have some fun tomorrow, Master!'

Pink-Whistle went to see the Wobbly-Man after he had had his tea. The Wobbly-Man nodded and smiled. He was always ready for a joke. He had no feet at all, only a curved base, and he got along by wobbling himself fast. Ha! He would give Sam a shock tomorrow!

'Nobody's ever knocked me over yet,' he said to Pink-Whistle, 'and nobody ever will! I'll be along tomorrow, Pinkie!'

The next morning Pink-Whistle gathered some fine holly out of his garden – two big armfuls. Then he sent Sooty to buy a balloon, a long one, not a round one.

He blew it up as big as ever he could, but he had to put a bit of magic into his blow because he wanted a rather big balloon. He stuck an old top-hat on it with glue and put a pair of old boots at the bottom, also stuck on with glue – very strong glue it was, too!

He slipped a walking spell inside each of the boots, and then draped an old brown coat round it – it really did look most peculiar!

Sooty began to laugh. 'I *must* come and watch!' she said. 'I really must! Please let me, Master!'

'Well, I shall want you to pick up the boots, coat and hat when Sam bumps into Mr Balloon and bursts him, pop!' said Mr Pink-Whistle. 'So you can come. First I'll walk along with the holly – then I'll tell the Wobbly-Man to do his bit – and then we'll set Mr Balloon walking along on his magic boots!'

At four o'clock the next afternoon the Wobbly-Man, Mr Pink-Whistle, Mr Balloon and Sooty were all waiting for Sam. The children came out from school in a bunch that afternoon, because that was the only way they could stop Sam from bumping into them. He was too much of a coward to tackle a lot of children together.

Sam was cross. Blow! Wouldn't some child run home alone? Well, he would hide and see. So, as usual, he slipped into a doorway and watched.

The children ran down the street – and then, when there was nobody there, Sooty whispered to Pink-Whistle.

'Now's the time to begin, Master – I can see Sam watching from that doorway.'

Mr Pink-Whistle slipped out of his hiding-place and began to walk down the dark street. Sam saw him – and thought he was a child, because Pink-Whistle was small. He raced out of the doorway and ran behind Pink-Whistle. Just as he was about to bump him, Pink-

Whistle swung round with his armful of holly!

'Ooooooh! Ow!' yelled Sam, finding his face and hands pricked with the sharp holly. 'What is it? Oooh, I'm hurt!'

He stopped to nurse his hands and feel his face. Whatever had that child been carrying? Then he saw the Wobbly-Man coming along. At least, he could just make out someone waddling towards him – who was it? Ah, perhaps it was old Fatty, who was in the form above him! Sam grinned.

He rushed at the Wobbly-Man and gave him an enormous bump. The Wobbly-Man wobbled over sideways and then wobbled back so violently that he gave Sam a sharp knock that nearly sent him flying! Sam was most surprised – and very angry.

'Don't you dare to fight *me*!' he said. 'I'll shove you right over, see?' And he gave the Wobbly-Man another tremendous push that made him wobble to and fro very fast indeed.

Sam watched him, a sturdy wobbling shadow in the dark street. Why didn't *Fatty* fall over? He pushed hard again, but all he could do was to make the Wobbly-Man wobble faster and faster.

'You're not Fatty!' cried Sam, suddenly

frightened. 'You're not! Who are you? I don't like you. Stop wobbling, do stop wobbling. I won't push you again, I promise.'

But, of course, the Wobbly-Man had to wobble, no matter where he went, and Sam watched him wobble away into the darkness, wondering whatever he was.

'Funny!' said Sam to himself. 'Very, very funny. Most peculiar. Anyone would think that that fellow couldn't walk, the way he wobbles as he goes. I don't like it. I'll just give someone else a good shove, and I'll go home.'

So he waited. The next person that came down the dark street was a tall man. Sam didn't dare to run and bump into him – no, tall men had a habit of reaching out and giving him a jolly good shake!

Ah – here was someone coming – someone short, with a silly top hat on his head. Sam grinned. Whoever it was that was coming was walking very near the holly hedge – it would be fun to push him right into it. Let someone else feel what it was like to be pricked all over! Sam's hands were still sore with the scratches they had had.

Of course, it was Mr Balloon this time!

Pink-Whistle had set the spell going in the boots, and the long-shaped balloon, dressed in old top hat, old coat and boots was now walking down the street.

'It's just a silly old tramp,' said Sam, catching sight of him in the light of a lamp. 'I'll give him such a shock – one of my very BEST BUMPS!'

So he ran from the doorway where he

stood and bumped into the Balloon-Man. He shoved him hard against the holly hedge – and all the prickles ran into the balloon. BANG!

San nearly jumped out of his skin. He stared at where the old tramp had just stood – but he had completely disappeared! Sam couldn't see the top hat, boots and coat lying in a little heap half-under the hedge.

'Ooooh! He's gone! He went BANG and disappeared!' howled Sam. 'What have I done? What's happened! Help! Help!'

The Wobbly-Man, who had wobbled back on the other side of the road, and had joined up with Pink-Whistle again, laughed till he cried. Pink-Whistle laughed too, and Sooty ran to collect the hat, boots and coat.

Other children heard Sam's calls for help and ran up to him. 'What's the matter? What's up?'

'I bumped into somebody and got pricked all over, look!' said Sam, and he was actually crying! 'And then I bumped into somebody else, and he wobbled over and wobbled back and hit me – he was horrid! And then I bumped into a silly old tramp with a top hat – and he went BANG and disappeared. I'm frightened!'

'Serves you right,' said a small boy. 'Now all you want is someone to bump into you and you probably wouldn't *ever* shove people about again!'

The children went off together, grinning. They didn't feel in the least sorry for Sam – it would teach him a lesson!

Sam went down the street too, sniffling miserably. He didn't mean to bump into anyone else he met that evening! What with pricks and wobbles and bangs, he had had quite enough.

Someone padded behind him. Someone soft bumped violently into him! Over went Sam and rolled into the same patch of mud into which he had bumped so many others. He sat up and yelled.

'Sooty!' said Pink-Whistle's voice. 'Sooty – you shouldn't have bumped into him like that – you really shouldn't. Look how muddy he is!'

'I couldn't help it!' said Sooty. 'Really, Master, but he'll *never* bump anyone again!'

Sooty's right – and do you know, when the children heard all about Sam's strange adventures the next day, one boy looked very wise, and said:

'It rather sounds as if old Mr Pink-Whistle was around last night, Sam. You'd better be careful!'

Now, however did he guess?

Chapter 5

Mr Pink-Whistle Gets a Letter

One day a letter popped through Mr Pink-Whistle's letter-box.

Sooty the cat picked it up and took it to her master.

'A letter for you, Master – marked URGENT,' said Sooty.

'Ah,' said Pink-Whistle. 'It looks as if it is from a child – so it certainly *is* urgent.'

He opened the letter and read it out aloud to Sooty:

'Dear Mr Pink-Whistle,

'I do hope this gets to you. I'm a little girl called Katy, and I live with my mother. We haven't much money, but we have a nice lot of hens, and they lay eggs, which we sell.

'But somebody comes and takes the eggs. We

303

don't know who it is, but it is very serious for us because we do need the money we get for the eggs. We hardly have any to take to market now.

'You go about the world putting wrong things right, dear Mr Pink-Whistle. Do you think you can put *this* right?

Your loving friend,

KATY.'

'P.S. – I know about you because of the stories I've read.'

'What a nice little girl she sounds!' said Sooty. 'Will you help her, Master?'

'Of course!' said Pink-Whistle. 'I'll go along this very day. Look up a bus to – let me see, what's the address – Tipkin-on-the-Hill. I've never been there before.'

Sooty went off to get the bus timetable, and soon Mr Pink-Whistle had discovered the bus that went to Tipkin-on-the-Hill. He put on his hat, said goodbye to Sooty, and set off. Nobody took much notice of the funny little man on the bus, except two children who noticed his pointed ears and green eyes.

'He's like Mr Pink-Whistle!' whispered one to the other. 'Oh – suppose he *is*!'

Mr Pink-Whistle didn't say a word, he just twinkled at them. Then he suddenly made himself invisible – and the two girls stared at his empty seat in surprise. They didn't know that he had got up very quietly, tiptoed to them, and slipped big bars of chocolate into their school-bags! How exactly like Mr Pink-Whistle to do a thing like that.

When he got to Tipkin-on-the-Hill he went

to find Katy. She was feeding the hens, and they were clucking round her – cluck-cluck-luck-luck-cluck! Cluck-cluck-luck-luck-cluck! Then the cock stood up straight and crowed. He had suddenly seen Mr Pink-Whistle, and he knew him.

'Cock-a-doodle-doo! We're pleased to welcome YOU! Cock-a-doodle-doo!'

'Good morning, Katy,' said Mr Pink-Whistle, and the little girl swung round at once. She stared in delight.

'Oh! You've come! Oh, you really are Mr Pink-Whistle, aren't you?' said Katy.

'Yes, I really am,' he said. 'I'm sorry to hear of your trouble. Tell me about it.'

Katy told him. 'Somebody comes and takes the eggs at night – and often in the daytime, too! Our cottage is lonely, as you see – and when I'm at school and Mummy is at work, anyone can slip in here and steal the eggs.'

'I'll find out who it is,' said Pink-Whistle. 'Don't you worry any more. Are your hens laying well?'

'Not very,' said Katy. 'So we can't spare the ones that are stolen! Oh, Mr Pink-Whistle, fancy *really* seeing you! I never, never thought you really *would* come!'

'I can't *always* come when people are in trouble,' said Pink-Whistle. 'But I happened to have nothing to do today. Now – isn't it time you were off to school?'

'Yes, it is,' said Katy. 'I shan't tell anyone at school about you, Mr Pink-Whistle, or they'll all be out here to see you – and you'd never be able to find out who the thief is. But I don't know *how* I'm going to keep such a wonderful secret!'

She ran off to school and left Mr Pink-Whistle in the hen-run. He turned to the hens and the big, beautiful cock. 'Cluck-luck-luck!' he said, speaking the language of the chickens. 'It's my belief you know the thief. Cock-a-doodle-doo, tell me who – who – who!'

The chickens all talked back at once, clucking and cackling loudly. Mr Pink-Whistle nodded. 'Thank you, I'll give him such a fright!'

The little man went into the hen-house and shut the door. He made himself quite invisible, sat down in the corner and waited. Nobody was about at all. Katy's mother was still out at work, and Katy was at school.

The hens clucked and cackled together in

the run outside. Then suddenly the cock crowed loudly, and Mr Pink-Whistle listened.

'Cock-a-doodle-doo, a visitor for *you*!' Then the door of the hen-house opened and someone crept in. It was quite a shock to Mr Pink-Whistle to see the thief so well-dressed – he had expected someone down-at-heel and ragged.

'So this is Mr James Pinch, the thief,' thought Pink-Whistle, watching the smart-looking young man as he went to the nesting-boxes one after another and took the eggs there. He slipped them into his big pockets, and then crept out again. Pink-Whistle followed silently.

Mr Pinch went to a big house and in at the kitchen entrance. Pink-Whistle followed.

The man came to a woman in a big white apron, who was bending over a great stove.

'Here you are, Cookie,' said the young man, and he handed her out the two dozen eggs or so that he had in his pockets. 'That's one pound fifty, please. All new-laid! I bought them in the market.'

Dear, dear – what a story-teller! Pink-Whistle shook his head and made up his mind that this young man wanted a shock.

And Pink-Whistle would give him one – oh, yes, a very peculiar shock that would teach him a lesson, too!

Mr James Pinch went off to his room to change into his uniform. He was a footman and waited at the table of Lord and Lady High-Up. Pink-Whistle went with him, and sat on his bed, quite invisible, while he changed his clothes.

'Cluck-luck-luck!' said Pink-Whistle, sounding exactly like a hen. 'Cackle-cackle-*squawk*!'

The young man was extremely startled. He jumped and looked round. 'Cackle, cackle, cackle,' said Pink-Whistle, exactly as if he had laid an egg and was proud of it.

Mr Pinch felt really most alarmed. He looked under the bed for any hidden hen. He looked behind the chest.

'Cock-a-doodle-DOOOOO!' said Pink-Whistle, just behind him. The young man almost jumped out of his skin.

'What is it? Where's that hen – and now a cock!' he said, angrily, feeling very scared. 'There's nothing here – not even a feather.'

'CLUCK!' said Pink-Whistle in his ear, and the young man rushed out of his room in a fright. He tore down the stairs and into the kitchen. The cook was there, and the maids, and the butler, all talking together.

'What's up, Jamie?' said the cook, as the young man rushed in, panting. Before he could answer, Pink-Whistle began clucking again. 'Cluck-cluck-cluck-cluck-CLUCK! Cluck-cluck-cluck-cluck-CLUCK!'

'A hen! A hen in my kitchen!' said the cook, and took up a broom to chase it out. 'Where did it come from? We have no hens here!'

But she couldn't find it, of course, Pink-Whistle sat on a chair and chuckled to himself. Then he began again.

'Cackle, cackle, cackle – CACK! Cack-cack-cack-CACKLE!'

'There now – it must have laid an egg!' cried one of the maids. 'But where is it? Is it in the larder?'

The larder door was opened, and Pink-Whistle slipped inside, bending down under the shelf, still quite invisible.

'Cock-a-doodle-DOO!' he crowed as loudly as he could.

'Well, if there isn't a cock about now, too,' said the butler. 'I never heard of such a thing! Where *are* the creatures?'

'Look here – we'd best not waste any more time in looking,' said the cook. 'My dinner will be late, and then My Lady High-Up will have plenty to say!'

Pink-Whistle took a rest. He waited till the footman went into the dining-room at dinner-time, to wait on Lord and Lady High-Up. Then he went, too, still invisible. He stood just behind Jamie Pinch.

'CLUCK!' he said, right in Jamie's ear. 'Cackle CACKLE! Sqqquawk!'

Jamie jumped and dropped the dish he was holding. CRASH! The butler frowned, and so did My Lady. Jamie picked up the bits and ran from the room. Pink-Whistle ran behind him. 'Cock-a-doodle-DOO!' he crowed in delight. Poor Jamie nearly fell over in fright. He looked round for the cock but there wasn't one there. He took another dish from the cook and hurried back. Pink-Whistle hurried after him.

'Cluck-cluck-cluck!' said Pink-Whistle, just behind Jamie, as he came into the room. The butler swung round angrily. 'Jamie! What are you thinking of? Stop doing that!'

'But – but – but,' said Jamie, just exactly at the same moment as Pink-Whistle said, 'Cluck-cluck-cluck!' So it sounded as if Jamie were clucking!

'Get out of this room,' said Lord High-Up. 'Any more of this nonsense and you'll lose your job.'

'Cock-a-doodle-DOO!' crowed Pink-Whistle at the top of his voice, and Jamie rushed out of the room. Pink-Whistle went, too, following him very closely.

'Here comes Jamie again!' said the cook. 'What's up with him? And bless us all – there's that cackling noise again! Where's it coming from? Jamie, do *you* know anything about it?'

'No, I don't!' said Jamie, looking very scared at the loud, cackling noise just near him. 'Everywhere I go, I hear it.'

'It must be something to do with *you*, then' said the cook. 'We didn't hear it when you were in the dining-room. Sometimes it's a hen, sometimes it's a cock!'

Pink-Whistle obligingly became both. 'Cluck-cluck, cock-a-doodle, cackle-cackle, doo!' he said, clucking and crowing loudly. Jamie gave a scream and ran into the scullery.

'Cock-a-cluck-a-cackle-doodle-doo!' he heard just behind him, and sat down with his head in his hands. What a dreadful evening – but it hadn't ended yet. Pink-Whistle clucked and clacked, cackled and crowed – and once he forgot himself and did some very lifelike quacks as well! Jamie thought he must be going mad. He went up to his bedroom and lay down.

Some feathers were coming out of a hole in his pillow. Pink-Whistle smiled to himself and pulled out a handful. Then he sat down on the floor and pretended to be a hen and a cock fighting. He scrabbled on the floor –

and then suddenly flung the feathers up into the air.

Jamie watched in alarm. Now these awful creatures were fighting – tearing feathers out of each other. He groaned and shut his eyes. 'I'll *never* go near a hen again!' he said.

Pink-Whistle spoke in his own voice then – a very solemn, deep and stern voice. 'Who steals eggs? WHO steals eggs? And then he gave the answer, crowing like a cock. 'Cock-a-doodle-doo! It's you, you, YOU!'

'Oh, who is it?' said Jamie in alarm. 'Tell me, tell me! I'm sorry, very sorry, and I'll never do it again. I'll give Katy all my savings to make up for what I've done.'

'Do, do, DO!' said Pink-Whistle, pleased.

'Do, DO!'

Jamie got up and took a money-box from a cupboard. He slipped out of his room and down the stairs. He ran all the way to Katy's, with Pink-Whistle close beside him.

Katy was just shutting up the hens, looking sad because eggs had been stolen again that afternoon. Jamie rushed up to her and put the money-box into her hands.

'Katy! I stole your eggs – I've stolen them for a long time, even though I knew you and your mother were poor. Please forgive me. I'll never do it again. See, I have brought you all my money.'

Katy was too astonished to say a word. She took the box, and Jamie at once ran off again. How glad he was not to hear any more clucking or cackling or crowing in his ear that night. What a fright he had had!

Mr Pink-Whistle!' said Katy, in a low voice. 'I know it's all because of you! Mr Pink-Whistle, are you here? I want to thank you.'

'Dear me, I forgot I was invisible,' said Mr Pink-Whistle, and immediately said the words that made him visible once more. Katy saw the dear little fellow standing there, beaming at her, and ran to him.

'Take half the money!' she said. 'Oh, how clever you are! What did you do?'

'The money is all yours and your mother's,' said Pink-Whistle. He told Katy what a fright he had given to Jamie, and the little girl laughed till she cried. 'Oh, I wish I could have heard you!' she said. 'I do wish I could!'

'It was very funny,' said Pink-Whistle. 'I really enjoyed it. I'm glad you wrote to me, Katy dear – I do like to put wrong things right, as you know.'

He kissed her goodbye and went, humming a little song.

> 'Cock-a-doodle-doo,
> I've lots of things to do,
> When things go wrong
> I come along
> And see what I can do.
> Yes, I see what I can do,
> Cock-a-doodle-doo!'

I really do like Mr Pink-Whistle, don't you?

316

Chapter 6

Well Done, Mr Pink-Whistle

One afternoon, when Mr Pink-Whistle was enjoying a little nap in his garden, his cat Sooty came up to him.

'Please, Master, wake up,' she said. 'There's a little girl come to see you, and she says it's important.'

Pink-Whistle woke up with a jump. 'A little girl – important?' he said, blinking at Sooty. 'Bring her here at once. Little girls are always important to me – and little boys, too!'

So Sooty brought a little girl of about nine years old to Pink-Whistle. She gazed at him shyly. 'I hope I haven't disturbed you, Mr Pink-Whistle,' she said. 'But I managed to get your address from a little boy you once helped.'

'And what have you come to see me for?'
asked Mr Pink-Whistle. 'Sooty, bring some
lemonade and your new buns.'

Sooty ran off and came back with a tray of
home-made lemonade and chocolate buns.
'What a lot of buns for only two people,' said
the little girl.

'But surely you can eat five or six new-made
chocolate buns!' said Mr Pink-Whistle. 'Help
yourself and tell me what you've come for.'

'Well, it's about a boy called Peter,' said the
little girl, taking a bun. '*Peters* are usually nice,
but this one isn't. In fact, he's really horrid,

and you see, nobody can do anything about him. So I thought perhaps you could.'

'Well, you know, I don't like people to tell tales,' said Pink-Whistle. 'Are you sure you ought to tell me about this Peter? And tell me your name, too please, I'd like to know.'

'I'm Geraldine,' said the little girl. 'Oh, aren't these buns nice! Did Sooty really make them? You know, Mr Pink-Whistle, I've read all about you in a book; that's how I know that you go about the world trying to put wrong things right. And I think that's a lovely thing to do.'

Pink-Whistle liked this little girl. He was sure she hadn't come just to tell tales. He poured her out some more lemonade.

'I'll tell you about Peter,' said Geraldine. 'It isn't really telling tales. The other children all asked me to come to you for help.'

'Well, tell away,' said Pink-Whistle, 'and do have another bun. Eating always helps talking if you've got something to say, and I can see you have.'

'Oh, do you think that, too?' said Geraldine. '*I* always think so. Well – Peter is a big boy at our school, and he hasn't got a bicycle. Most of us have, but he hasn't.'

319

'Go on,' said Pink-Whistle.

'So he borrows ours,' said Geraldine. 'He never *asks* us if he can – he just takes them. He rides nearly all the way to his home on them, then jumps off, throws them into a hedge and walks the rest of the way home.'

'I see. And whoever owns the bicycle he has taken has to catch the bus home,' said Pink-Whistle.

'Well, no – because usually we haven't the bus-money if we ride bicycles,' said Geraldine. 'So we have to walk home and we're late and get scolded. We get scolded about our bikes, too. But nobody can stop Peter. We don't like to tell tales of him to the teacher, or to our mothers – you see, Mr Pink-Whistle, he's very big and strong.'

'I see,' said Mr Pink-Whistle again. 'Do have another bun. Sooty will think you don't like them if you leave any. I suppose this Peter does quite a lot of other things besides taking people's bicycles.'

'Oh, yes,' said Geraldine. 'But I needn't bother you with those. You can guess them.'

'I think I can,' said Pink-Whistle. 'Pulling hair – slapping – pushing and pinching – all the things a big boy does when he's a bit of a bully. But I suppose what you want my help for is about this bicycle business.'

'Yes, please,' said Geraldine. 'Last week Jimmy was given a lovely new bike for his birthday and promised to keep it clean – and two days ago, Peter borrowed it, and left it out in the rain all night in a hedge. Now Jimmy's father has taken his bike away for a month because it looks dreadful!'

'Well, I think I can cure Peter,' said Pink-Whistle. 'Tell me the address of your school, please. And do have another bun. Don't waste them!'

'I've *never* tasted such lovely buns,' said Geraldine. 'But I'm not going to take the last one, thank you very much.'

She said goodbye and shook hands. Pink-Whistle took her to the gate, thinking how nice it was to meet children with good manners. You just couldn't *help* liking them!

Next morning Pink-Whistle made himself invisible, as he often did, and went along to find Geraldine's school. Ah – there it was – and there was the bicycle shed. Pink-Whistle looked at the bicycles – what a lot! Plenty for that bad boy Peter to choose from!

Pink-Whistle went down the row of bicycles

rubbing each back wheel and muttering something. Ah, he knew plenty of useful spells! He stood up straight and smiled. Now Peter, look out! If you take a bicycle today, you'll be sorry!

Well, Peter did, of course. He was out before any of the other children and ran to the shed. He picked out Benny's because it was nice and shiny. He was out of the school gate before anyone could stop him, riding at top speed!

He went down this road, and that, on his way home – and then suddenly he looked astonished. He ought to be in Hacking Road – but he wasn't. He was in a road he didn't know at all. How could he have taken a wrong turning? He turned round and rode back to the corner. There was a signpost there that Peter didn't remember at all. He stared at it in surprise. It pointed four ways.

One way said '*To Mr Whack.*' Another said '*To Hard Work Village.*' A third said '*To The Dragon*' and the fourth said '*To The Crosspatch Witch.*'

Peter couldn't understand it. He had never in his life seen the signpost before. He didn't want to go to any of the people or places it pointed to. Good gracious! What was he to do? Had he lost his way?

He couldn't stay by the signpost all day so he got on his bicycle again and rode off in the direction of *Mr Whack*. He didn't like Hard Work – he didn't want to meet a Dragon – and he certainly didn't like the sound of the Crosspatch Witch! He didn't much like Mr Whack's name, either!

He was not at all pleased with Mr Whack when he found him! He rode down the lane, round a corner, and came to a small house. He jumped off, meaning to ask his way home.

He knocked at the door – and out came a big man with a whippy little cane!

'Ha!' he said, 'I'm Mr Whack, and I'm glad you've come to see me. I've heard about you. You take bicycles, don't you? Hold out your hand!'

Peter didn't want to, but his hand held itself out – and then the other hand held itself out, too. Whack, whack, whack – how that whippy little cane enjoyed itself! But Peter didn't. Like all bullies, he was a coward, and he howled loudly.

'There – that's what happens to bullies,' said Mr Whack. 'Leave the bicycle. I'll see that it's returned to its owner. Go over that stile, and you'll see the way home.'

Peter went off, still howling. He climbed over the stile, and went across the field. When he came to the other side he found, to his great astonishment, that he was in the lane that led to his home. He simply couldn't understand it.

He didn't take anyone's bicycle the next day. His hands smarted too much to hold bicycle handles! But the day after he took Geraldine's! He raced out of the school gates on it, laughing to think of the little girl's anger and dismay when she found it was gone.

And will you believe it, the bicycle took him to the same signpost as before! There it stood, its four fingers pointing to *Mr Whack, Hard Work Village, The Dragon*, and *The Crosspatch Witch.* Peter stared in horror.

How had he come here again? He couldn't imagine! Well, he wasn't going to Mr Whack this time, that was certain. But he didn't want to go to Hard Work Village either – or to the Dragon or the Witch.

He decided to take the road that led to the Dragon. 'It can't possibly be a *real* dragon,' said Peter to himself. 'There aren't any dragons now. It must be a hotel called the "Dragon". I'll ask there for my way home.'

But, you know, it *was* a real dragon! As Peter rode on round the corner, he saw a gate right across the road, and beside it was a cave. He got off his bicycle to open the gate – and suddenly out of the cave came a dragon.

He looked very like the one that St George fought long ago, but he had remarkably kind eyes.

'Wait!' he called, in a roaring voice. 'Are you good or bad?'

'What do you mean?' said Peter. 'And who

are you? I don't believe in dragons. You're just somebody dressed up!'

'I'm not,' said the dragon. 'Ah – now I know you. You're Peter, the boy who takes bicycles, aren't you?'

Peter began to feel as if he was in a bad dream. 'No, I don't take bicycles,' he said quickly. 'Let me go through this gate, please, whoever you are.'

'I can't,' said the dragon. 'Not until I've fought you.'

'What do you mean! I don't fight dragons!' said Peter, scared.

'Well, you see, I'm a good dragon,' said the dragon, 'so I fight bad things and bad people. *Bad* dragons fight good people. You're bad, so I must fight you. Look out for yourself!'

And the dragon ran at poor Peter, who turned and fled for his life! The dragon sat down and laughed. He was rather disappointed too. He really was a very good and kind creature, and hadn't had a fight for years, but sometimes he felt he *would* like to hit out at something bad.

Peter fled down the road and came to a little wood. He saw a path there and raced down it, afraid that the dragon might be following him. And quite suddenly he came to a part he knew – how strange! Why, just down there and round to the left and he would come to a road he knew quite well! *How* had he managed to get to that strange signpost again?

Peter was very, very puzzled when he got home. What a horrid adventure! Why did the bicycles keep taking him to that signpost instead of to his home? Was there a spell on him? He didn't believe in spells, but certainly something peculiar was about.

He remembered that little Geraldine had said she was going to ask Mr Pink-Whistle for help. Well, he didn't believe in any Pink-

Whistles either. But suppose – just suppose Geraldine *had* gone to him, wasn't this just the kind of thing that Pink-Whistle would do?

Peter went out into the garden to think. Should he ask Geraldine if she had found Mr Pink-Whistle? No, she wouldn't tell him anyway.

'Oh, I wish I knew what was happening to me!' groaned Peter. 'Why do those bicycles take me the way I don't want to go? I believe it's all something to do with Mr Pink-Whistle. I'd tell him a few things if he were here!'

'Well – I *am* here,' said a quiet voice, and suddenly, in front of Peter, Mr Pink-Whistle appeared bit by bit – first his head, then his hands and legs, then his body. It was really very strange. Peter didn't like it at all.

'Now tell me whatever you want to,' said Pink-Whistle. 'I'll listen.'

'No, I don't want to say anything,' said Peter.

'Not even about bicycles?' said Mr Pink-Whistle. 'I wonder whose bicycle you will take tomorrow, Peter – and where you will go? You're having some adventures, aren't you? You must enjoy taking those bicycles from the other children!'

'I don't! I don't! And I won't any more, either!' cried Peter. 'I won't go to those horrible places, so it's no use your putting spells on the bicycles. I'll never touch one again! Never!'

'Peter! Who in the world are you talking to?' called his mother, coming into the garden. At once Mr Pink-Whistle disappeared, and was quite invisible. Peter gave a gulp and ran indoors up to his bedroom.

Well, as you can guess, Peter never took anyone's bicycle again – and will you believe it, when his father offered him one of his own for his birthday, he said no!

'What! You've been pestering me for a bicycle for *three* years – and now I can buy you one, you say no!' said his father. 'You don't mean it, surely?'

But Peter *did* mean it, and you can guess why he didn't want one. He was afraid it would take him to that peculiar signpost again!

Chapter 7

Mr Pink-Whistle and the Scribbler

One day, when Mr Pink-Whistle was sitting in his garden, he saw the front gate open, though he could see nobody there.

'Now, what –' he began, in surprise – and then he saw a tabby cat slip through the gateway, shut the gate behind him, and run to the back door.

'Ah – a friend of Sooty's, I suppose,' thought Mr Pink-Whistle, and turned back to his book. Before he had read two pages, Sooty, his cat, came walking out to him, and behind him came the tabby cat, looking rather shy.

'Mr Pink-Whistle,' said Sooty, 'this is a friend of mine – Paddy-Paws. He is a very good and honest cat – but he is most upset because somebody has been scribbling lies about him on a wall.'

'Dear me!' said Pink-Whistle, in surprise. 'Well, Paddy-Paws, I wouldn't take any notice of that.'

'It isn't so much himself he has come about as his little mistress, Fanny,' said Sooty. 'This boy who scribbles on walls writes horrible things about Fanny, too, and they make her cry. Paddy-Paws says she's sweet and kind, and he's most upset about it. He wants to know if you can help him.'

'Yes, Mr Pink-Whistle,' said the tabby, finding his tongue suddenly. 'You do put wrong things right, don't you?'

'I try to,' said Pink-Whistle, 'But what is it you want me to do, Paddy-Paws?'

'Well, sir, stop this boy from scribbling more horrible things,' said the tabby cat. 'I'll take you to the wall he scribbles on and you'll see the dreadful things he writes. Everybody can read them, sir, and they get very upset. But this boy is big and strong, and nobody can stop him.'

'Well, I'll come along now,' said Pink-Whistle, and he shut his book, 'Lead the way, Paddy-Paws!'

So Paddy-Paws led the way. Over a field, across a stile, down a lane, through a small village, along a high road and into another village. Pink-Whistle padded along with him. Sooty had been left behind at home.

Paddy-Paws came to a wall – and there, written in different coloured chalks, were a great many horrible sentences. Pink-Whistle read them out loud. '"Betty is a cry baby. Katie is a tell-tale. George is a cowardycustard."' Pink-Whistle began to frown. 'Dear, dear – what things to write for everyone to see! Most unpleasant!'

He went on reading. '"Fanny is a thief. She took my rubber at school. Paddy-Paws is a thief, too. He steals fish from the fish shop."'

'I never did steal fish, you know,' said Paddy-Paws, pulling at Pink-Whistle's trousers. 'And my little mistress, Fanny, isn't a thief. She's honest and truthful and good. And Betty isn't a cry baby – but she can't help feeling miserable when her tooth aches, can she? And George isn't a coward, and –'

Pink-Whistle frowned as he looked at the rows of nasty writing on the wall, and read on further – '"Old Mrs Brown is mean. Nancy cheats at sums." Good gracious me, what an unpleasant person this boy must be!' said the little man. 'What's his name, Paddy-Paws?'

'Harold, sir,' said the tabby cat. 'Look – here he comes, with one of his bits of chalk!'

In a trice Pink-Whistle made himself invisible. Paddy-Paws stared round and about in surprise. Where had this nice little man gone to so suddenly?

'I'm still here, but you can't see me,' said Pink-Whistle, in a whisper. 'You go home now,

Paddy-Paws, and leave this boy to me. I'll soon cure him.'

Pink-Whistle went up close to Harold's back, and watched what he was writing. Harold wrote very clearly and quickly. 'Ellen took some apples off Mr Henry's tree when he wasn't there.'

Just as he was finishing this, a boy and girl came up. 'Hello, Ellen!' said Harold, with a big grin. '*I* saw you up that apple tree. You're a bad girl!'

Ellen gave a scream when she saw what Harold had written. 'You horrid boy! Mr Henry *said* I could pick six apples because I fed his hens for him. And oh, look, George, he has written that you're a coward. Fight him!'

But George, the boy with her, was very small, much smaller than the big Harold. He stared at Harold, and tried to speak boldly. 'You're NOT to write things like this, you're –'

But he didn't say any more, because Harold knocked him right over, bang, wallop! Ellen pulled George up to his feet and they both ran away at once. Harold was too big to fight!

When Harold left the wall and walked away,

whistling, Mr Pink-Whistle followed him, still invisible.

He was quite surprised at all the things that Harold did on his way home.

He slipped into Mr Henry's field and took three pears growing on the wall there. He went into old Mrs Brown's garden and cut her washing-line so that all the clean clothes fell to the ground. He chased a small kitten up a tree and then threw stones at it.

Pink-Whistle was amazed. To think that a bad boy like this dared to write horrible things about other children, where everyone could read them! He followed Harold very closely indeed. What was this awful boy going to do next?

Harold walked by the greengrocer's shop. Outside were boxes of all kinds of goods. Harold took a quick look round to make sure no one was about and quickly picked up two bananas. He put them under his coat. Pink-Whistle could hardly believe his eyes!

Then Harold saw a small boy walking down the road and ran quietly behind him. He snatched the boy's cap off his head and threw it over a garden hedge up into a tree. The boy swung round fiercely, but when he saw

Harold, he said nothing. Harold was so big and strong!

Pink-Whistle watched everything that Harold did. He followed him all the way home and indoors. He saw him tiptoe to the larder and take two jam tarts. He saw him take some chocolates out of his mother's box. What a dreadful boy!

Soon Harold's mother came home from her shopping. 'Hello, dear,' she said, 'have you had a nice day at school?'

'Yes,' said Harold. 'I was top in class. The other children are so stupid. Katie's a tell-tale, and Fanny is a dreadful thief, and George is an awful coward.'

'Your father will be pleased to hear you were top again,' said his mother. 'Here he comes. Put the kettle on for tea, Harold.'

Pink-Whistle stood quietly in a corner behind the couch, out of the way of the family as they got tea and sat down to it. Then the little man crept out of his corner, still invisible, and put his hand into the right-hand pocket of Harold's coat. He pulled out some pieces of coloured chalk. Ah – Pink-Whistle was going to have a fine time now!

'Fanny is an awful thief,' said Harold,

eating his bread and jam. 'She stole my rubber yesterday and today she took my best pencil.'

Just as he finished, there came a faint squeaking sound from the big bare wall opposite the table. It was made by the red chalk that Pink-Whistle was suddenly using to write with!

Everyone stared in amazement as a line of very neat writing began to appear on the wall. The words followed one another fast.

'Harold is a thief. He stole two bananas from the greengrocer's shop. He stole three pears from Mr Henry's wall-trees. They are in his pockets now.'

Harold's father stared at the writing in the greatest astonishment. 'What's all this?' he said. 'Who's written that? Have you *really* stolen pears and bananas, Harold?'

There came another line of writing.

'Harold is a coward. He knocks down children smaller than himself. He is cruel. He chased a tiny kitten up a tree. He is unkind. He threw a small boy's cap over a garden hedge.'

Harold sat glued to his chair, his eyes following the strange writing that went on and on across the wall. He began to whimper, because he was so frightened.

'Harold is a cry baby,' wrote the chalk. 'Look at him whimpering now! He took two jam tarts from the larder. He stole two chocolates from the box over there. He –'

Harold gave a loud cry and rushed over to the wall, pulling his hanky out of his pocket as he ran. He rubbed it over the wall, so that it smudged and blurred the writing.

But Pink-Whistle immediately went to the next wall and went on writing there!

'Harold cut Mrs Brown's washing-line

338

and made all the clothes fall to the ground. He –'

'Oh! Harold – surely that wasn't *you* who did that!' said his mother. 'Mrs Brown told me someone had cut her line – oh, Harold, what is all this writing? Who is doing it?'

'It is Mr Pink-Whistle,' wrote Pink-Whistle. 'I have seen the wicked things that Harold scribbles on walls, so I am doing the same to him. But the things I write are true, and what *he* writes is untrue!'

'*Mr Pink-Whistle*!' said Harold, in fear. He had read many tales of the little half-brownie man, and he knew all about him. He snatched the chalk as it wrote, and felt round and about for Pink-Whistle – but he was safely behind the couch again, still quite invisible!

Pink-Whistle gave a little laugh. 'Beware, Harold!' he said. 'Whenever you write on walls outside, I shall come and write on your walls here. If *you* can do it, so can I!'

And with that he skipped over the couch, went to the window and jumped neatly out. He set off home, longing for a cup of tea. Sooty was most interested to hear all that had happened!

'Now, Sooty, I want you to go each night

and see if anything is written by Harold on that wall,' said Pink-Whistle, drinking a nice hot cup of tea. Sooty nodded. She went that very night, with Paddy-Paws – but, dear me, someone had been along and wiped the wall clean!

'That's Harold!' said Paddy-Paws. 'I saw him go by with a duster. I guess he won't ever scribble on walls again, Sooty!'

For a whole week Sooty went to look at that wall, but it was as clean as could be. Harold wasn't going to have Pink-Whistle coming along to his home and writing things about *him*! That wasn't funny at all.

Paddy-Paws was very grateful. He caught three rats in Pink-Whistle's garden and laid them in a row on his front doorstep to show him how grateful he was. Pink-Whistle was surprised to see them there!

'Thank you, Paddy-Paws,' he said. 'I'm always pleased to put wrong things right, you know. Tell me, if you want my help for anyone, another time!'

He's nice, isn't he? I'd love to have a friend like old Pink-Whistle!

Chapter 8

Mr Pink-Whistle's Cat is Busy

One day, just as Mr Pink-Whistle was about to go and catch the train to visit his old aunt, Sooty, his cat, came running to him.

'Master – there's a black cat with white paws come to see you. He wants your help.'

'Well, Sooty, I can't miss my train,' said Pink-Whistle. 'See if you can help him. After all, you're a cat too, and you know my ways – you can surely put right whatever the cat has come about. You can use anything out of my spell-cupboard if you like.'

'Thank you, Master,' said Sooty, and waved goodbye to Pink-Whistle from the door. Then she shut it and went to the back door where the black cat with white paws was waiting patiently.

'*I* will put things right for you,' said Sooty, rather grandly. 'What's the trouble, Whiskers?'

'Well, it's the man next door,' said Whiskers. 'He's a thief, Sooty, and a very sly one. He only takes small things, usually what he can put into his pockets, or carry in his hands. I've known about him for years, of course, but I've never bothered about him till today.'

'Why today?' asked Sooty, taking the cat indoors. 'Help yourself to the milk in my saucer – it's nice and fresh. Now tell me everything!'

'Well, I belong to a very kind old lady,' said Whiskers. 'But she's going a bit blind, and she can't see as well as she used to – and this man next door – Mr Gubbs his name is – keeps coming in, pretending to ask how she is – and each time he pops something into his pockets – perhaps a sausage roll from the larder, or a book from the bookshelf, or even something from my old lady's purse.'

'How wicked!' said Sooty. 'Just because the old lady can't see!'

'Yes. And this morning my old lady missed the stick she uses when she goes for a walk,' said Whiskers. 'It's a fine black one made of ebony, with a shining silver handle, and she's very proud of it. Now it's gone.'

'Did this Mr Gubbs take it?' asked Sooty.

'Of course he did! He came in to see the old lady this morning, and patted her hand, and asked her how she was – and told her not to come and see him out of the door, he knew the way all right – and he took the stick out of the hall-stand. He thought nobody saw him – but *I* saw him! I was sitting in a dark corner of the hall, watching.'

'It's a pity you aren't a dog,' said Sooty. 'Then you could bark at him and bite him.'

'I've tried hissing loudly, and putting out my claws if he comes near me,' said Whiskers.

'But he kicks me, and I'm afraid of him. Wouldn't Mr Pink-Whistle help? He likes to put wrong things right, doesn't he?'

'He's gone away. *I* can help instead,' said Sooty. She went to Mr Pink-Whistle's cupboard and looked at all the strange bottles and boxes there. She suddenly caught sight of a small bottle with blue-green liquid inside, and she laughed. She took it down.

'Look,' she said, 'this is a funny spell – it makes any tongue talk, and –'

'But that's silly – tongues always do talk,' said Whiskers.

'Not *all* tongues!' said Sooty. 'Not the tongues of shoes, for instance! Look, Whiskers, if you can manage to rub this spell on the tongues of Mr Gubbs' shoes, they will soon chatter away and tell the world about him – and *he* won't know who's doing the talking!'

Whiskers laughed so much that he fell into the saucer of milk. 'Give me the bottle,' he said. 'I'll manage to spread the spell on the tongues *somehow*. Oh, what a time I'm going to have!'

He hardly waited to say goodbye to Sooty, but ran off with the bottle in his mouth. And that night, when Mr Gubbs was in bed, and his shoes were in the kitchen, waiting to be cleaned, Whiskers hopped in at the kitchen window and ran over to them. He poured a little of the blue-green liquid over the tongues of the shoes, and then rubbed it in.

'Now talk, shoes, talk as much as you like when Mr Gubbs wears you,' he mewed. 'Tell the world about him and what he does!'

Well, next morning, Mr Gubbs put on his shoes as usual, and wondered where he could go that day to pick up a few more things that didn't belong to him. Yes – he would go round the market. It was market-day, and there would be plenty of chances for him to take this or that.

So off he went. On the way he met Mr Jaunty and managed to take his nice, blue silk handkerchief out of his pocket as he passed by. Then, when he passed Miss Jinky's house, he saw a lovely pink rose blossoming by the wall, and he snipped it off and put it in his buttonhole.

At the market he wandered round, smiling at people he knew, nodding politely, and stopping to say a few words to this person and that. He also managed to pocket half a pound of butter when Mrs Plump, who owned the butter stall, wasn't looking, and to put a handful of ripe cherries into his pocket.

Then little Nicky and his sister came by and he offered them each a cherry from the ones in his pocket. 'Oh, thank you!' said Nicky. 'Are they out of your garden?'

'Yes, I picked –' began Mr Gubbs, but another voice interrupted him. 'He took them from the cherry stall,' said the voice. 'Oh, he's clever, he is!'

'Pooh – call that clever?' said another voice. 'I call it cunning – sly and cunning!'

Mr Gubbs was extremely startled. He looked all round for the talkers, but there was no one near except the two children, and *they* were looking most astonished. They gave him back the cherries at once and ran off.

'Now look here – who said that?' began Mr Gubbs and heard a peculiar husky laugh somewhere near. It came from the tongue of his right shoe, but he didn't guess that, of course.

He went on his way, feeling puzzled and soon met Mr Burly, the farmer.

'Hello, Gubbs!' said the farmer. 'Do you want to buy fresh farm butter? Go to my stall and –'

'He doesn't want any,' said a small voice, loudly. 'He's got some in his pocket – it's a bit squashy.'

'He took it from Mrs Plump's stall when she wasn't looking,' said another voice. 'Oh, he's an artful one! He wants watching!'

'Er – good morning,' said Mr Gubbs to the astonished farmer and hurried off, his face flaming red. *Who* was it talking about him like this? He looked behind him. Was it some irritating children who had been following him? No – there was nobody near.

Old Lady Smiles came bustling up. 'Oh, good morning, Gubbs. My word, that's a beautiful rose you have in your buttonhole. What's its name?'

'Er – I think it's called Beauty,' said Mr Gubbs. 'I – er – picked it from my garden this –'

'He picked it off Miss Jinky's best rose-bush when he passed by her garden this morning,' said a little voice, quite clearly. 'Nobody was looking.'

'You can't believe a word he says!' said the second voice. 'Not a single word. Horrible old Gubby!'

The other shoe-tongue gave its husky little laugh. 'What about the blue silk hanky? I saw him take it out of Mr Jaunty's pocket. Did you?'

'Oh, yes! I've just as good a view as you have of all his goings-on,' said the other shoe-tongue. 'I remember when –'

'Good morning to you, Gubbs,' said Lady Smiles, stiffly. 'I don't know if you can hear what I can hear – but I must say that I think it's all very extraordinary. *Good* morning!'

It soon got round that there was something peculiar about Mr Gubbs that morning, and to his great distress one person after another came up – just when he didn't want them! He must, he really *must* find out about those voices! As for the shoe-tongues, they had a perfectly marvellous time!

'Look – there's Mrs Grocer coming – she doesn't guess that old Gubby took a tin of

biscuits from her shop last week! Hoo-hoo-
hoo!'

'And here comes old Mr Woosh. What
would he say if he knew that Gubby took his
tin of tobacco and popped it into his pocket,
when he went calling on him the other day?'
said the other tongue. 'It's no good his asking
for it back either – it's all gone up in smoke!'

'Hoo-hoo-hoo!' laughed the other voice.
'You are very funny this morning. Ooooh, I
say, look – here comes the policeman – and
Gubby doesn't like the look of him!'

Indeed Gubby didn't! He was now so
scared of what the extraordinary voices were
saying that all he wanted to do was to run
back home, shut his door and hide. But the
policeman had been very, very interested in

some of the things that the market-folk had told him about Mr Gubbs, and he wanted to make a few enquiries.

Gubby began to walk away quickly, and the voices shouted loudly, 'He's scared! He knows he's got that butter in his pocket!'

'And his socks belong to Mrs Jinky's husband – he took them off the line the other night!'

'And he took the vest he's wearing, too! And what about his watch? Wouldn't the policeman like to know about that! Hoo-hoo-hoo!'

Mr Gubbs took to his heels and ran, panting hard, hoping that the policeman hadn't heard a word. If only he could leave those voices behind! They must be somewhere in the market, nasty, mysterious voices. Once he got home he wouldn't hear them any more.

But he did, of course! As soon as he was indoors and the door shut, he sat down, out-of-breath – and the first voice began again.

'He can run fast, can't he? My word, I got quite giddy, going up and down, didn't you?'

'Yes, I did. We shall have some more fun soon, though – the policeman will be along, and a few others. Old Gubby's going to get what he deserves at last, the mean old fellow. I never did like him, did you?'

'Why – it's my *shoes*!' shouted Gubby, and he took them off and ran out into the back-yard. He took off the dustbin lid and threw in the shoes. Then back he went and put on his slippers. They had no tongues, thank goodness!

But it's no good, Gubby. There's a tramping down the street, and soon there will be a knocking at your door! You'll have to answer some very awkward questions, and when your house is searched you will find yourself marched off to the police-station. So shiver in your slippers, Gubby – the time has nearly come. Ah – rat-a-tat-TAT!

Sooty, Mr Pink-Whistle's cat, was longing to know all that had happened, and she was very glad to see Whiskers coming along the next day, looking as if he were bursting with news.

'Sit down. Tell me everything!' said Sooty, and Whiskers began. He told the whole story – he related everything that the shoe-tongues had said, and he told how Gubby had at last been found out and taken to prison.

'How do you know all this?' asked Sooty,

wiping tears of laughter from her eyes. 'Did you follow Gubby to market?'

'No. But, you see, he threw the shoes into the dustbin and I heard them talking to each other there, and went to rescue them. I took them out of the dustbin and they told me everything that had happened – every word they had said, and I laughed till my whiskers nearly fell off!'

'Where are they now?' said Sooty.

'Oh, they thought Mr Pink-Whistle might like to lend them to someone else some day,' said Whiskers. 'So they walked here with me. They're outside the door. Thanks very much, Sooty, for helping to put a wrong right all by yourself. My mistress has got back her ebony stick and she is very happy.'

And off went Whiskers, grinning, very pleased with himself. 'goodbye,' said a shoe-tongue as he passed the shoes. 'You certainly did us a good turn when you rubbed that blue-green polish into us – we've never had such a fine time in our lives. Thank goodness we don't belong to Mr Gubbs any more.'

'Nasty old Gubby! Hoo-hoo-hoo!' said the other tongue.